THE BRAND OF VINDEX
THE COMPLETE ADVENTURES
OF CAPTAIN VINDEX

THE BRAND OF VINDEX

THE COMPLETE ADVENTURES OF CAPTAIN VINDEX

TRACY FRENCH

COVER BY
LEJAREN HILLER

POPULAR PUBLICATIONS · 2023

TABLE OF CONTENTS

VENGEANCE OF VINDEX

*Their Leader Was the Avenger Who Called
Himself Vindex, and They were Men
Without Fear or Mercy, Fighting Gangland's
Most Terrible Traffic—Kidnaping!*

1

THE MEN WHO HAD LOST

FROM THE HEAD of the table Captain Vindex surveyed
his four recruits in grim appraisal. They looked as hard and
impassive as marble. Their eyes were icy, their expressionless faces formidable. Altogether, they suggested men who
would be violently contemptuous of either life or death.

One by one they had been ushered into the main room
of the penthouse on top of the tall office building at Broadway and Twenty-seventh. Each in turn had nodded silent
recognition to his host and had taken one of the chairs
placed at the big mahogany table. Between themselves
they now exchanged glances of guarded scrutiny, indicating them to be so far mutually unacquainted.

"When I invited you to join me in a crusade of vengeance
and extermination against the kidnaping racket," began
Captain Vindex slowly, "it was only after a year of tracing,
investigating, testing and discarding hundreds of victims
such as ourselves. What I sought was a few select associates
who had been hardened to adamant in hell-fire, men who
were too strong to crumble into slag or ashes. Men unable
to forget and eager to repay—as keen as tigers for the hunt
and as hungry for the kill. Men who, unhampered by hypo-
critical scruples, would help me in carrying on a ruthless
counter-reign of terror among the snatch gangs preying

on thousands of helpless homes. For that all lawful methods are utterly inadequate either to prevent or to suppress
or to punish them, we know to our bitter personal cost!"

"Well, here we are," spoke one of them harshly. "And
ready to go!"

Paying him no attention, Captain Vindex continued: "So
that I knew you intimately before you ever saw me. After I
had finally chosen and enlisted you, I had to persuade each
of you to accept his prospective associates on trust for the
time being. But the reason for that was obvious."

"Reasonable enough in my case," said the firmly knit and
finely finished man at his left. "The devil himself couldn't
have known me better. I realized that if you had been able
to turn *me* inside out that way, your judgment of the others
ought to be equally trustworthy."

"I figured too that you must know what you were doing,
Captain Vindex," agreed the big, hard-faced man seated at

*His hand remained
tucked into his armpit*

his other side. "In any case, your proposition listened to me as welcome as water in the desert. It is something I wanted to do. It makes life worth dying for!"

"Makes death worth living for, he means," barked the second man at the left side of the table, a man tall and spare, whose graying hair showed rusty traces of original red and whose long, strong fingers closed and unclosed in front of him with a sinister flexion. "I don't know how you discovered me for what I am; but I swear to God, the mere hope of taking some personal revenge for the blood, the tears, the torment that I suffered and still suffer, makes me live again!"

The fourth man, dark and sharp-featured and soberly

"The reason you're not dead," said Vindex, "is that one can't extract poison from a dead snake."

buttoned up in black at the table's foot, shrugged his shoulders and smiled faintly, as if the thing went without saying.

"Very well," Captain Vindex tossed out an oblong leather box some four inches in length, of a type made to contain a small piece of jewelry. "Look at that."

The man of the flexing fingers reached out and drew it to him. It gaped open at the pressure of his thumb. A thick ringlet of yellow hair, freed from compression, seemed to crawl over its edge on to the table. On the bed of white satin within the box remained another object, all the more gruesome because it was so small—a child's finger. Around the finger, between its raw severed end and its second joint, was a thin circle of gold.

"IN GOD'S NAME, what's that?" huskily asked the opener.

"It purports to be the finger of Lora Perham," replied Captain Vindex evenly. "The hair is hers, according to microscopic tests. And the ring is hers."

"Lora Perham?" frowned the hard-faced man at his right. "And who's Lora Perham? Another snatch? I hadn't heard of it."

"No, because a warning left at the scene promised instant death to her if any information was given out. Lora Perham is the four-year-old daughter of a wealthy Broad Street importer. She was kidnaped five days ago from her home in Westchester. The threat was pinned to the seat of a tricycle she had been riding up and down the Perham driveway. The tricycle was found just outside the gate. Evidently the snatch was made from a passing car. The kidnaping of Lora Perham was in any case to have been the occasion of our first meeting here tonight, though I'd expected to have more time to organize our campaign. But somebody appears to be forcing our hand."

"Any trouble about the ransom?"

"So far The Voice has made no sign at all," answered Captain Vindex. "They're undoubtedly letting Perham stew until he gets soft. He can pay. He has plenty."

"But, my God! Then why *that?* Usually they don't do that sort of thing except to put the screws on when people don't come across quick enough!"

"There was also a note in the box, typewritten on a strip of cheap paper. Let me read it: 'If you want the rest of the kid back whole, at any price, call off Captain Vindex.'"

"The hell!" said the hard-faced man softly.

"So the poor fool talked!" exclaimed the man opposite.

"He did not talk," said Captain Vindex. "Except to me, and not until I'd forced his hand, having had some previous intimation of the kidnaping."

The man at the foot of the table stirred. They all stared.

"Though not till too late to prevent it," went on Captain Vindex. "Then I persuaded Perham to let me take hold. He could hardly do otherwise. His secret was out. But that box is the first communication of any kind they have sent him since the snatch. It was delivered at his office late today after he'd left, and I opened it. So he hasn't seen it. I'll add," said Captain Vindex significantly, "that Perham does not know me in my present undisguise, or by the name of Vindex. Except to you four that name is wholly impersonal. A name without a body."

"So!" said the hard-faced man slowly, looking around the table. "Then we're all suspect."

Captain Vindex shrugged. "More to each other than to

me, possibly. But as you know, until tonight I've deliberately withheld from you all knowledge of each other's true identities as well as of my own. If one of you should have got cold feet and decided to back out before we met, the knowledge might easily have proved a menace to the rest of us. Now, however—" he glanced toward the little box and its grisly contents, "we exchange credentials at once and in full."

"I'LL SAY WE do!" agreed the other emphatically. "Full names and stories! Everything!"

"Everything," repeated Captain Vindex. "I'll begin. I used to be an actor. After a number of years I became popular and I made money. Too much money. I was married and had two children, a boy and a girl. One night my wife and I returned from the theater to find the nursery empty. They'd been kidnaped. I would have paid any ransom, I'd have sold body and soul to get them back. But the hue and cry raised by the police drove the kidnapers to cover, and all that was ever found of my children was their dead bodies in a cellar over in Jersey. Their mother soon died of grief. That was my end as a member of my profession, as a member of civilized society. My name—"

"Arnold Brent!" broke in the hard-faced man. "Great God, I worked on your case!"

"So you did," shrugged Captain Vindex. "But without result. One of a thousand proofs of the utter uselessness of the police in such cases."

"Arnold Brent!" echoed the second man on the left side of the table, whose nervous fingers were still at work strangling phantoms. "I hadn't recognized you! Yet we—yet I've seen you twenty times—years ago, I mean. I was once called back stage out of the audi-ence when some member of your company had an accident, a sprained ankle. You—"

"Yes. But I doubt if you'd even recog-nize your other self if you met him, Doctor. However, the alteration in our

Vindex

looks which helps to disguise us will prove useful, since we shall do our killing *incognito* and under cover. All the advertising to be had out of our war to the death on the snatch racket is to accrue only to the name I've adopted, *Captain Vindex.* That name will serve for all of us!"

"Vindex! The Avenger! The sign and seal of a bloody retribution!"

"Just that." Captain Vindex turned to the man at his immediate left. "Number Two?"

"I was a lawyer," spoke the man addressed, without a change in the bleak expression of his face. "My wife was about to have a child—our first—when she was kidnaped. Negotiations started, but the police blundered in and she was never returned to me. Months later she was found buried in a makeshift grave somewhere up the river. She and her stillborn child. My name was Thrale, Edwin R.,— when it happened down on Long Island three years ago. That's all."

Captain Vindex looked to his right.

"Thrale. I remember that one too," said the man with the hard face quietly, watching his own forefinger trace idle patterns on the board. "Me, I was already at war with those devils, as you know. Name's Steve Burns. Used to be in the D.I. of the Department of Justice. Back in thirty-two I was assigned to the snatch racket. Maybe I rushed 'em too hard. Anyway, I had a boy of six my wife had died to give me. One day he was tricked out of his school an' run off with. Not for ransom—me with only a government salary—but for revenge, as some hellish letters soon made plain. Weeks later he was sent back to me. Dead. In a trunk and in pieces. The whole Division never could get a line on the bloodthirsty fiends."

Captain Vindex glanced down the table across the little box. Standing open under the light, with the fragment of baby flesh bedded on its white satin lining, it looked startlingly like a miniature coffin ready to be closed for final interment.

"Doctor?"

"Ellsworth!" responded Number Four in a voice that rasped like a file. "Robert Ellsworth is the man I used to be. Surgeon here in town, country place up in Westchester. My two little girls, five and three, were stolen one evening while my wife and I were dining out. We never saw them again. Their mother finally lost her mind from grief. Then, thank God, she died too! I didn't. I've lived a thousand years since I lost them—all of them!" he exclaimed fiercely. He sunk his face in his hands.

"What about the ransom?" said Burns.

"I paid it! Sixty thousand dollars, through a hole in a

door to somebody in the dark, though the police did their damnedest to prevent my getting in touch with the kidnapers at all. Maybe I didn't, maybe it was—too late!" He pointed at the box. "Who knows but worse than that may have happened to them before the end," he said hoarsely. "I've dreamed of it till sometimes I think I'm a little mad!"

"Perhaps we're all a little mad," said Captain Vindex. "If we are there's good reason for it. But our madness will be more than atoned for by saving others from what we've suffered ourselves. Number Five?"

2

THE MAN FROM THE DEAD

"ACTON," RESPONDED THE man in black. "I am Reuben Acton. You may have heard of the Acton case out in San Bernardino two years ago."

"Check," nodded Burns. "I wasn't on it but I read about it."

Acton threw him a swift glance. "Then you know," he went on smoothly, "that my house was entered one night through the baby's bedroom window with the intention of kidnaping her. The deed had been threatened, so she was always guarded. She slept with a nurse in the room. I woke up, thinking I'd heard a noise, and went out into the hall, where I was struck on the head and knocked unconscious, so that I saw nobody and knew nothing. I didn't come to until next day. But the mother—my wife, I mean—must also have heard something, for she too got up, and ran to the child's bedroom. The nurse, it seems, had been drugged. The other servants, sleeping down stairs, had all been seized and tied up, except for a Japanese house-boy who came running when my wife screamed for help. Then—one of the intruders lost his head and began shooting. The mother, the child, and the houseboy, all were killed. The slayers got away."

"Pretty tough," deprecated Burns, not unsympatheti-cally. "Yet maybe the rest of us wish to God we had nothing worse to look back on. Let's see, you're a minister, aren't you, Mr. Acton?"

"I was," admitted Acton carefully, "though I'd retired when I moved to Bernardino. Why do you ask?"

"Well, Reverend, I just wondered. Because I judge we're due to shed blood in considerable quantities. At least, I hope so."

"You can count on Mr. Acton," intervened the cold voice of Captain Vindex. "I expect his assistance to prove invaluable."

Burns spread his hands.

"That settles that, then," he conceded. "No offense intended. Brother Acton can understand I was just a little surprised at the combination, that's all."

"But how about the question of who gave away the name of Captain Vindex?" asked Thrale. "Isn't that what we're after?"

Captain Vindex rose.

"We'll summon another witness," he said briefly. Then he disappeared through a door behind him.

FOUR MINUTES LATER a different figure slouched back into the room. Wary eyes whipped over the expectant quartet. Then a quizzical sneer strained the loose lips of it, while one hand waved a casual greeting toward the table in general. The other as casually remained concealed in the side pocket of a suit of clothes that would have made a hit on Grand Street.

" 'Lo there, Chief. Well, look who's here! Hyah, Fed', you still foolin' yourself?" The voice too, was Grand Street.

"Damn," muttered Steve Burns without moving. "It's Foxie Gordon!"

Acton leaned forward at the far end of the table, his hands gripping its edges till his knuckle bones showed white. His eyes bulged in their sockets as he stared at the unpleasant apparition.

"Hell!" he breathed hoarsely and unclerically. "Hell!"

The startling figure straightened and shook itself together, quick fingers playing about its face. "Did you think hell had opened?" spoke the voice of Captain Vindex. "You're wrong. Once in hell they stay put."

"Captain Vindex!" exclaimed Burns, relaxing. "You must be the devil himself!"

"A role I've adopted," said Captain Vindex grimly, removing further traces of his make-up. "I hope to be successful in it!"

"Well, that was some impersonation! You could put it over almost anywhere. For that minute you *were* Foxie Gordon!"

"I had years of experience in quick imitations and character parts of all types. Gordon was easily revived. He may yet prove useful to us."

"Who *is* Foxie Gordon?" asked Ellsworth.

"I can give you the dope on that louse," growled Burns. "He used to be on my books; that's why I knew him. A cheap gangster, a killer an' a kidnaper's punk too; though we never could hang anything on him." Suddenly he looked down the table. "Say! If I remember right, Foxie Gordon was suspected of bein' mixed up in the Acton case! He was known to be out on the Coast that year!"

"That's why I was startled for a moment," Acton

answered the battery of eyes aimed at him. He had recovered his composure. "The police tried to get me to identify him by his pictures at the time. As I had seen nothing, I couldn't. But I recognized him here—the impersonation, I mean—from the pictures."

"You certainly looked as if you saw a ghost," Thrale said. "I happened to notice you."

"Mr. Acton had strong personal reasons for believing that he did see a ghost," said Captain Vindex in his meticulous monotone. "Foxie Gordon was found dead in Van Cortlandt Park this morning. He'd stopped a clip of thirty-eights with the back of his head."

For a few seconds there was silence while the subtle implication crept into the open. Thrale got it first.

"What? You mean Acton could have known—*did* know that Gordon had been killed?"

"By God!" Steve Burns banged a fist down. "I *knew* something was ticking in that dumb brain o' mine! Even if he didn't know Gordon was bumped off, he knew a lot too much about that night in Bernardino! Knocked cold at the start-off an' with everybody else too dead to tell about it, how would he know that *one* of those two guys lost his head an' did the shooting, f'r instance? Tell me that!"

Acton still sat rigid, staring as if overwhelmed. But suddenly his blank eyes blazed and his right hand flashed up and underneath his coat. Simultaneously there came a flat explosion from the other end of the table. Acton's body jerked, and his hand, instead of reappearing, remained tucked into his armpit as if it had been pinned there.

"The reason you're not dead," said Captain Vindex icily as he laid down the gun, whose muzzle still breathed hot smoke, "is that one can't extract venom from a dead snake. You're going to spill your secrets before you die. Take a look at his hand, Number Three."

BURNS WALKED DOWN the table, turned Acton's coat back over his shoulder and lifted the man's numbed arm away from his body. "Bull's-eye. Got him right in the back of the hand as he grabbed his rod. Judas, what a shot!" Deftly patting Acton's pockets, he straightened up to exhibit a flask. "That's all he's heeled with, except for a hipload of rye."

"Give him some. Doctor, there's first aid stuff in the drawer in front of you. Fix up the hand, please. I want him to talk."

"Keep right on wanting," said Acton shakily, as he lowered the flask left-handed. "Want and be damned!"

"What's your name?" clipped Captain Vindex. "Who are you?"

"Reuben Acton!"

"Who was murdered with the rest of his family two years ago. Did you mean to say *Floyd* Acton?"

No answer.

"No great matter," Captain Vindex shrugged. "Where you'll be planted they don't bother about headstones."

"Floyd Acton—who's he?" asked Burns.

"He was Reuben Acton's brother—born crook and grown devil. For years merely a cheap family bloodsucker and a disgrace to his name. Finally, with Foxie Gordon, he planned a big-time cleanup, the snatch that turned into a slaughter. When Gordon made his getaway, Floyd Acton remained in that house of death, disposed of his brother's body, and for two weeks posed as Reuben Acton, who was

Thrale

Ellsworth

Burns

a newcomer to Bernardino and still scarcely known there. It was possible because of a close resemblance between them and because Floyd did himself up in bandages and pretended a natural state of shock. Then he cashed in on all the property and slipped away to Chicago to turn professional on the strength of his two newly discovered amateur talents."

"Meaning what?" demanded Burns.

"Meaning his gift for acting a part and his gift for major crime," replied Captain Vindex. "Still posing as Reuben Acton, who had to stay alive, you see, he pretended to turn missionary to the underworld as a Christian reaction to his wrongs. In reality, under the sobriquet of The Parson, he began the systematic reorganization of the kidnaping racket into a smooth-running devilish big business."

Dr. Ellsworth dropped the bloody hand he was bandaging and raised both of his own, his fingers writhing. "Is this man—this fiend the one you called Floyd Acton, Captain Vindex?"

"Not a chance, Doctor, in spite of his assumption of the Acton name. The Parson's far too astute to have ventured himself here. He may be after information, but he's not picking his own chesnuts out of the fire. So go ahead with your dressing."

Burns said: "Looks to me like he'd have to go some to beat you collecting information, Captain Vindex. How in the name of all the devils—" his eye flicked to the lower end of the table and he checked himself. "You would not want to tell it now, though. Or would you?"

"Why not? Dead men carry no tales. Part of what I've told you I learned when I was exploring the underworld myself, hunting for my own crucifiers. The Parson was already a big shot for the mob to boast about. What little I know about the Perham kidnaping I got from Foxie Gordon—and paid him well for it."

THE MAN WHO called himself Acton looked up sharply, and with staggering assurance. "And you'll get a laugh out of how that ape Gordon put himself on the spot!"

"Yes?" returned Captain Vindex. "And how?"

"By laying a pretty little paper picture of his double-cross right into my hand! Do you get it? By asking me to change him a double-X—a twenty—out of the wad you'd paid him, and I recognized it by the number of the bill. So I saved fifteen smackers," he sneered. "All I gave him for it was five ones."

"In the back of the head."

"You guessed it," snarled the killer. "And now, since we know all about each other, it's a draw. Let's talk terms."

"What terms with a dead man?"

"I'm not dead yet," warned the other. "And if you know so much, you'll know I'm not taking any chances. I've still got my ace in the hole!"

"Meaning Lora Perham. Well, where is she?"

"Wouldn't you like to know! Well, I'll tell you this much. If I shouldn't be back at a certain place by midnight it'll be just too bad for little Lora Perham. She'll be cold meat within the next five minutes. Pretty near eleven, now, isn't it? Go ahead and shoot if you feel that way. Take your own choice."

"It's your choice, not mine," said Captain Vindex calmly. "A choice between a quick death by shooting if you talk and a death long drawn out by extreme torture if you don't. A leaf out of your own book."

A harsh murmur from around the table that sounded perilously like approval shook the gangster's equanimity for a moment, and his eyes dropped to the little finger in the box. But he quickly reassured himself. "Oh, no, you wouldn't," he decided. "Not your kind. Besides, I meant exactly what I said about the Perham kid. That was all planned beforehand. So I'll call your bluff."

Captain Vindex clapped his hands. From the door behind him entered a stocky Japanese, who bowed and hissed politely.

"Kato, gentlemen. Kato was with me fifteen years as dresser and valet. After the children came he appointed himself their nurse and guardian. He loved them only less than myself. Kato possesses Oriental ideas concerning the administration of vengeance and the ability to translate them into very effective ferocity."

Kato smiled broadly and bowed again. Captain Vindex turned to him, decisively. "Three of these men, Kato, are friends and allies. Men who have suffered as we have, and who are as hungry for revenge as you and I. *That* man"—he pointed at him—"is a stealer and a killer of little children. He has just helped to steal another one as he might have stolen ours, and he refuses to tell what he has done with her. He must talk. But he must live until he does talk. And later I may need his face. You understand?"

"I un'erstan'. You want make up like him. I get out color, hair, clo' like him for you," said Kato.

"That's it. See what you can do with him."

"Sank you," bowed Kato, smiling. "I do. He talk."

Still smiling, but with the glare of a stalking tiger, Kato approached his victim. There was a brief whirlwind, but no real struggle. In spite of the strength still left in the gangster's muscles his arms were pinned behind his back, his hands were wrenched upward toward his shoulder blades. Then, sweating with excruciating pain, he was walked Spanish through the door that led into the unknown regions of that mysterious penthouse.

The door closed behind him.

3

KATO PAYS A DEBT

CAPTAIN VINDEX SAID: "I hope we'll have time enough."

"Are you sure he wasn't bluffing to save his life?" asked Thrale. "You think they'll really kill her if he doesn't show?"

"I doubt if he'd have come without that protection. Even when he found himself practically on the spot he evidently expected to get away whole in return for Lora Perham's life."

"We should have accepted the bargain," frowned Thrale. "Her life is more important—"

Steve Burns shook his head. "Listen. If that devil was to be let go knowing we four, she wouldn't have a chance. They'd kill the kid quick an' make a break for the woods."

"Without any question," nodded Captain Vindex.

"Then pray God your man Kato knows his business!" jerked out Dr. Ellsworth. "Why didn't I wring that hellhound's neck? My fingers itched to do it!"

"Yes, an' s'pose you had, then where would we be—or the kid, rather?" said Burns gravely. "Captain Vindex, who *is* that fake Acton? And how'd you happen to invite him to sit in?"

"It's quite simple. Reuben Acton had been on my list of prospects for investigation. He was supposed to be still living, you remember. When I discovered the facts in the case I dropped him. But recently I saw Foxie Gordon here in town, and—as an old pal who'd known him in Chicago, of course—I picked him up. Gordon was gabby and told me that The Parson—Floyd Acton—was also here, in connection with some big snatch to be pulled off. He couldn't or wouldn't tell me the name, however. So I managed to trick him into tipping off The Parson that a fool called Vindex was enlisting men for a war against the snatch racket and that it might pay to look into it. Which he, The Parson, in his Reuben Acton personality, could easily do.

"The Parson fell for it, sending the same dummy to represent himself whom he had employed in accepting the invitation."

"Not so dumb, either," said Burns. "He strutted his stuff all right at first, an' he talked like a college professor. And he was sure too smart for Foxie Gordon."

"The Parson's no fool," warned Captain Vindex. "He's building up a powerful organization and he's staffing it with a regular Brain Trust. He'll give us plenty of trouble."

"So that's where the leak was, about the name of Vindex," said Thrale quietly. "And you knew it right along."

"Of course. But I had to let you smell skunk in the trap for yourselves. If I'd acted sooner you might have taken me for a madman."

"By God," said Burns, "you're smooth! If you'd shot him for what he was when you first began to ride him, even, likely I would have. Yes, he was smooth too. But you were smoother."

"And don't forget that he's about the only possible source

of information as to Lora Perham's whereabouts. That was the big reason behind the invitation."

"The invaluable assistance you told us you expected of him," said Burns slowly. "Where was my brains?"

"Exactly. Well, that's all. Except that toward the end Foxie Gordon pretended suspicion or alarm. I had to sweeten his courage for him."

"And then he double-crossed you—no, the damned fool double-crossed himself, showing that marked bill to Acton."

"Not marked. The Parson's man claimed to know it by the number," said Captain Vindex. "But I didn't know the numbers of any of those bills myself. I had no occasion to take them. All I had asked the bank for was five hundred in tens and twenties."

Burns stared. "But then how in hell could this fake Acton have known them either?"

"That's the question. Something we'll have to look into."

THE DOOR OPENED. Kato entered smiling, to bow and hiss.

"He talk now," said Kato. "You want I bring him in?"

"Yes, bring him in."

Kato bowed himself out again, to return dragging his victim by the collar much as a tiger might drag its stricken prey. The killer's feet scraped limply over the carpet at the end of legs as limp. His arms hung downward like wet towels. But his eyes were wildly alive. At the end of the table Kato flipped his burden face up with a twist of his hand to plant it in the chair, sitting.

"Neck all right, face all right, tongue all right," said the

Japanese through his broad and imperturbable smile. "Can talk."

Captain Vindex frowned at his three awestruck companions.

"Don't let this shock you," he said coldly. "Don't forget that this devil and his kind have caused more pain and grief than he could suffer or repay in a thousand years of hell. Don't forget that still another child awaits further mutilation and death unless we can act in time."

"You—you'll have to hurry," croaked the broken gangster in a ghastly voice.

"Number Two, cross-examine him. That's your line. I've got to get busy turning myself into his likeness."

Kato had already brought a makeup box and was adjusting a small mirror on the table.

Thrale rose and stalked down to stand over the crippled man who was slouched like a rag doll in the chair, ninetenths inanimate.

"Listen, devil. At the first refusal to answer, at the first lie, back you go to get worked over some more! You understand?"

Death hovering over the gangster's head and the ocean of hate that poured into his eyes clothed him with a certain dignity, grotesque and horrible though his appearance was.

"If—you—promise me a bullet," he said with difficulty, "I'll tell you—what I know. And much—good may it do you!"

"It's still a promise," interjected Captain Vindex, working on his portrait with his own face for a canvas.

"What's your real name?" demanded Thrale.

"Cantwell."

"What did you have to do with the kidnaping of Lora Perham?"

"Nothing—so far. I knew it was—being pulled off, that's—all. I was to be The—Voice when the time came."

"And where is she hidden?"

"I don't—know," croaked Cantwell, with a sudden glint of venomous triumph. "I can't—tell you, and that's the—truth! You'll have to—ask The Parson!"

Thrale turned threatening eyes toward Kato, standing by Captain Vindex. The latter's flying fingers stopped for a moment.

"That may be so," he said. "It would be like The Parson not to let his left hand know what his right was doing. Biblical, too, as well as practical," he added grimly. "And who peddled this job?" he flung at the gangster.

"Don't know—that, either."

"No? Then where did you have to be by midnight if Lora Perham wasn't to be killed by five minutes past? Isn't that the place where she's being held?"

"Told you I don't—know where she is. Place I was going is—house near end of—West Hundred and Fifteen—close to Drive. Closed and—boarded up. Don't know—number."

"Seems to me there's one hell of a lot this bird don't know," rumbled Steve Burns. "Listen, guy, how about some numbers you *do* know? Like the numbers on the bill Foxie Gordon handed you an' you burned him down for? How'd you know *then?*"

Cantwell peered at Burns with a last distorted grin. "Too—late, smart cop," he gasped, his breath coming quick and short. "I'm—even—going to beat the gun! See you all—in hell!"

And he pitched forward on the table, face down.

THERE WAS AN instant of startled commotion. Dr. Ellsworth hauled the gangster upright into his chair and stooped over him. Then he straightened.

"Dead."

Slowly Captain Vindex turned to look at Kato. The Japanese was horrified.

"Dead?" he sputtered shrilly. "Oh, please excuse! But how can be? Only gave him portion of seventy-two disjointings punishment! Should live with, three—four days! Lose no blood; no break bones! Only muscle, only nerve!"

"Nerve!" muttered Burns. "No, you didn't break his nerve either. Damn! What do we do now?"

"We proceed," said Captain Vindex sharply. "All we have to go on is that Hundred and Fifteenth Street address, and I've got to make it by midnight as Cantwell. It may yet be where the child is hidden out, though it's not likely. Kato, hold up his head!"

Still shaking his own head, the Japanese supported that of Captain Vindex's deceased model with his hands. Finally Captain Vindex stood up and left the room, Kato silently following with the corpse flung over one shoulder.

Shortly, for the second time that evening, the living copy of a dead man walked back across the threshold.

"Well?" asked Captain Vindex in the voice that had been silenced. "How is it?"

Burns whistled. "Damn good—Acton—and that's no joke," he said soberly. "But I'm afraid it'll take more than first sight to get by in a case like this, Captain Vindex. You don't know who's who or what you're goin' to run up against. My vote is, we all go along together an' rush the joint."

"If Lora Perham *should* be there, the place will be guarded like the Bank of England. We'd never crash it in time to save her. The only possible chance is for me to attempt to get inside as Acton—as Cantwell, if that was his name. If he's really expected it ought not to be too difficult."

"Yeah. And then?"

Captain Vindex shrugged his shoulders.

AT TWELVE MINUTES to twelve a car rushed through One Hundred and Fifteenth Street and turned north on Riverside Drive. Three blocks up it returned to West End Avenue and headed south.

"Drop me at the corner and keep on going," said Captain Vindex. "Leave the car a few streets down and walk back separately. They may have eyes out. You can meet in the lobby of the big apartment house on the corner of the Drive; there'll be enough people coming and going to cover you. You saw the passage between the apartment and the house that's boarded up. If I don't join you by twelve-thirty you can try through the alley."

"O.K.," said Burns. "We'll be there."

Captain Vindex dropped from the left runningboard and walked casually toward the Drive. As he approached the closed old brownstone he studied its front. There could be no hesitation about trying for an entrance if he were being watched. All the windows were boarded blind, but there might be a peek hole in any of them.

The main entrance was completely covered by a false wooden front, built flush with the outer wall of the house. If there were a door cut in that false front he couldn't see it. In any case it would make too conspicuous an access to a closed house on a lighted and frequented street. He had his choice between a possible basement entrance under the stoop or a try at the rear of the house by way of the alley that separated it from the tall apartment on the corner of the Drive.

As he neared the stoop a quick glance up and down the block showed him that he was unobserved, at least from street and sidewalk. Vaulting an iron railing that ran right up to the stoop itself, he vanished into the dark under the stone arch. The basement entrance was also boarded up, and he didn't dare strike a match to find out if there were any way of circumventing its apparent impregnability. His fingers could feel no hinges, no crack indicating a door. But at last they brushed against the round knob of an old-fashioned bell pull set in the stone beside the wood.

Captain Vindex hesitated. But time was marching inexorably toward midnight. If Lora Perham were being held prisoner in that house and if The Parson's spy had told the truth about what was to happen to her if he shouldn't return by twelve, there was no time to waste. He knew only too well that The Parson would realize that both safety and success lay in living up to the last letter of the contract. That his every threat to kill would be carried out to the minute and to the last drop of innocent blood. For only that way could he maintain the necessary status of public and paralyzing terror that gave force to his threats.

So he had to be in that house on the stroke of midnight!

Twice Captain Vindex pulled the bell handle, laying his ear to the wood in an effort to hear some response. The house remained as silent as a tomb. He flung himself out, ran past the stoop and darted into the dark alley. At its end he could see starlight above a high wall. He sprang for the top, drew himself up and dropped on the other side into the ruins of an old garden. The rear of the house appeared to be as well protected against intruders as the front. But he found an ancient growth of ivy, its main stem thicker than his arm, climbing to the roof.

The acrobatic part of his long stage training stood Captain Vindex in good stead. He swarmed up the heavy mass of vine and at the top story discovered that the windows, instead of being boarded up, were merely shuttered. He reached and wrenched open a shutter, smashed a pane, unlocked the window and squirmed across the sill. He was inside the house at last, just as the chimes of the Riverside Baptist Church sang the hour.

The long-closed room was airless and unfurnished, and dust lay thick upon the floor. Every other room on that story and on the next below proved to be in the same condition. After probing every corner and closet, Vindex descended the main stairway to what in its day had been known as the "parlor floor," already partly convinced that The Parson's emissary had lied almost with his last breath. For there was no trace of recent human occupancy, even of the briefest. That meant, if the threat against Lora Perham had been authentic, that the child might already have been murdered somewhere, perhaps a hundred miles away. For it was now several minutes past twelve.

Nevertheless, Captain Vindex went on to complete his inspection, from the small reception room off the front hall to kitchen and laundry in the rear. There remained only the basement floor and the cellar. Another stairway brought him down into a short hall, at one end of which was the entrance from under the stoop. To one side opened a low room at the front. At the back of this room was another door.

Through it he stepped into a middle chamber. Just as he was on the point of swinging his flash around the room an iron blow knocked it from his hand. At the same instant he felt a lighter but more significant metal impact between his shoulder blades.

4

THE PARSON

EVEN BEFORE THE click of another flashlight created an immediate burst of brilliance to dazzle his eyes, Captain Vindex threw up his hands, for he knew that the snout of an automatic was boring into his back. But he disregarded the pair of punks standing to his right and left. Five feet in front of him stood a third man whom he could hardly fail to recognize as The Parson himself.

For The Parson was preposterously frock-coated and wore his collar backward over a high clerical vest, while from under the brim of a soft black felt his eyes gleamed balefully through eye-holes in a black silk mask.

The man at Captain Vindex's right suddenly stepped back and lowered his rod, staring at him.

"Hey!" he exclaimed. "Take a look! It's Canty we got."

"Keep that gat on him, you!" snapped The Parson. "Frisk him, Donovan!"

During the operation The Parson closely scrutinized its victim. When it ended he rubbed his soft white hands together, an oily smile playing over the visible portion of his face.

"Listen, boys," he said. "Like Moses, I sent one out to spy the land, to wit, Cantwell. One returns in his likeness, but ignorant of the necessary signal and of the proper entrance, he falleth into the pit he diggeth for others. Since Cantwell went forth to meet a certain Captain Vindex, said to have arisen like a serpent in our path, and as Cantwell seems to have fallen by the wayside, this then must be that same Captain Vindex, whom it more than ever behooves us to crush beneath our heel. For only the man who drew Cantwell's secret from him and slew him would have returned in his place with falseness on his face and in his heart. I know it, even without forcing him to wipe Cantwell out once again to prove it. Am I right?" he demanded peremptorily.

"I admit it," said Captain Vindex, without hesitation. "And I take it you're that devil called The Parson."

"Ah," beamed The Parson, "so the recognition is mutual. And since you have neglected the precaution so clearly set forth in Holy Writ—'Take heed to thyself, that thou be not snared by following them,' see Deuteronomy Twelve, Verse Thirty—I am to have the honor of officiating at your funeral, Captain Vindex."

"As I suppose you have already officiated at that of Lora Perham!"

"Not yet," The Parson surprised him. "If you hadn't arrived on time, even though in place of our poor departed brother Cantwell, my dear Captain Vindex, I'd have had to issue an order that might have cost us a small fortune. I say *might*, for there always exists the possibility of persuading anxious parents to pay sight unseen for treasures already laid up in Heaven. But now, since you have joined us, I can see no immediate need of our losing little Lora Perham. And as you yourself were the cause of her recent peril, Captain Vindex, it should afford you the greatest consola-

tion to realize that it is likewise to you she now owes her life. Unless, of course, the police should have been notified of her captivity."

"So far they've had no notice of it."

"And let us hope they continue to receive none, for little Lora's sake," smirked The Parson piously.

The Parson

Captain Vindex boiled at the brutal mockery, but a voice at his left helped to steady him.

"Well, Parson, how about it? Do I drill him? This damn gat's gettin' heavy!"

"No, you dumb ape, you don't drill him! We want no gunplay up here on the street level. Tie his hands and bring him below!"

So it was over. Attempting the conquest of Hell, he had fallen into the hands of the Devil before he could even strike a first blow. But it occurred to Captain Vindex that at least he needn't be dragged away to die like a steer at the slaughterhouse. A bullet sought was better than a bullet suffered. The Parson himself was holding a prudent gun on him while the two thugs seized his wrists to bring them together at his back for binding. Captain Vindex hunched himself for a desperate leap into the waiting lead, when a barrel from behind cracked down on his skull. He sagged, helpless, though not entirely unconscious. Even that last act of self-immolation was denied him.

HE RECOVERED HIS full senses in a place of chill and damp. His hands were tied tightly behind his back. Through the gloom lit by a flashlight and by a candle carried by The Parson he saw the common fixtures of a cellar—rusty pipes hung to the ceiling, bins against the shadowy walls, the ponderous front of an old-fashioned furnace looming at the further end. He was on the spot.

But The Parson led the way toward the furnace and disappeared behind it. Pushed along by his captors, Captain Vindex found The Parson unbarring a thick iron door in the end wall. A stealthy patter and rush, an eerie scuttling came to a silent end.

"The little creatures flee to their safe retreat," said The Parson amiably. "But they'll return as soon as they realize that instead of harm we mean them nothing but kindness." He held the candle high above his head to illuminate through the door a two-foot hole broken into the brick end of a small underground chamber three steps down from the cellar. "See?" he whispered.

Around the edge of the broken brickwork cautiously peered the head of an enormous rat. Another showed beside him. Then the velvet blackness beyond was pricked out with tiny pinpoints of light in pairs—eyes reflecting the faint illumination of The Parson's candle.

"God!" breathed one of The Parson's punks, "let's croak the guy quick an' get to hell out of here! They make me jumpy, them damn rats!"

The Parson laughed gently. "The little animals are even

more nervous than you are, Smoky. They're not used to human companionship. Not *yet!* However, you speak rightly. It's full time for us to leave and go back. Now that Captain Vindex is about to cease from troubling and prepares to take his rest, we must hasten to replace our departed associate Cantwell and go on with our program." He chuckled. "For without a Voice we're speechless, so to speak."

"*You* ain't," scowled his nervous henchman, "but I wish to hell you'd talk straight English, Parson. Howsomever, I guess I got part of it, though. Here goes!" He raised his gun.

The Parson struck it down. "I'll talk Dutch to you, you triple-damned blockhead!" he spat viciously. "And if you don't get that, I'll talk a language you do understand—*this!*" A stubby derringer leaped into his hand from a sleeve-spring, pointing straight at the startled gunman.

"F'r God's sake, Parson, don't!" spluttered Smoky, his face blanching in the candle-light. "I only thought—"

"With what—your feet? Don't try! I do the thinking—all you're hired for is to obey orders! Now take this candle and stick it up there on the wall!"

HE TURNED TO Captain Vindex with an instant change of manner. "You, at least, can understand me, my dear Captain Vindex. It's a pleasure to meet with real intelligence. What these fools don't seem to grasp is the fact that I should regret raising a hand against so clever a man as yourself—so I'll merely leave you here to entertain the rats. And if you should think to escape through a rat hole," warned The Parson, "let me inform you that that break opens only into what's left of a long-abandoned sewer extending well out into the river. It has now no other outlet, though it's alive with rats. Your candle may last you a couple of hours, but in the dark the little creatures get much bolder. So you should be picked to the bones before daylight."

At the top of the steps The Parson paused.

" 'And the carcasses of this people shall be meat for the beasts of the earth,'" he canted in his mealiest tones. "Meaning rats. See Jeremiah Seven, Verse Thirty-Three."

One of the punks glanced back at Captain Vindex with a look of horror. Then the iron door was shut, and Captain Vindex heard the heavy bars on the cellar side of it drop into their sockets.

He relaxed. From his first view of the ghastly little dungeon and the skulking picket line of rats, he had understood just what fate he was destined to, a fate far more dreadful than being shot. And yet at this moment he might have been worse off than he was. He might have been dead. Instead, he was still alive—and, if The Parson could be believed—so was Lora Perham.

Although his hands were tied, and most efficiently, Captain Vindex felt that he could keep the rats off for a time by kicking at them and stamping on them. At least, as long as his candle lasted.

The candle! He looked at it and a faint smile flickered over his lips. Rather foolish of The Parson to leave him a candle. A candle could be useful for other purposes than merely to see by. He took a step toward it. Then his little smile flickered out. The significance of the fact that the candle, stuck in its own grease on a protruding stone, stood inches above his head had at first escaped him. Now it became all too clear. The Parson hadn't been such a fool after all.

Without hands, how could he reach the candle to take it down? If he should knock it down with his head by jumping at it, it would most certainly go out, and then—Captain Vindex shuddered. Hundreds of foul-smelling rats running over his body to get at his flesh, burrowing into his clothing, cutting his tendons, rending at him fiercely, fighting and squealing for his tenderest parts while he couldn't even see to defend himself!

But hell! That was just the way The Parson wanted him to feel! Hopeless, horrified—

Captain Vindex put an iron clamp on his nerves and stared at the candle. Suddenly he turned to the hole in the wall and began to kick furiously at its edges. The astonished rats backed into the tunnel. Scraping together the broken pieces of brick, shoveling the debris across the floor with his feet, he managed laboriously to pile it against the wall underneath the candle. When the heap was high enough he stepped up on it, twisted his neck almost to a right angle, and delicately seized the candle between his teeth as close to its base as possible. He pulled carefully until it came loose from the stone.

Then, without daring to straighten his neck lest the flame eat at the candle and drown itself in melted wax, he stepped even more carefully down to the floor and lowered himself to his knees. He had to lie on his side to keep the candle upright and to wedge it in between two heavy fragments of brick. Next, with his lips he picked up smaller pieces from the pile and dropped them in place at each side of the candle to fix it more firmly in position. He used his chin to tamp the rubble, scorching hair and eyebrows freely in the process.

Finally Captain Vindex ventured to turn his back and feel for the flame with his bound hands. This, too, was an operation of the utmost delicacy. One false movement would mean the end. At last, judging by the fact that both wrists were being equally agonized by fire, he was able to maneuver the cord that bound them into the burning wick. He set his jaw and waited. All at once the cord parted. Twisting about, he saw that the candle still stood where he had fixed it. And it was still burning. But it was a long inch shorter than it had been in the beginning.

CAPTAIN VINDEX MOPPED the perspiration from his face, tied handkerchiefs about his burned wrists and considered his next move. He had no idea how long it had taken him to perform the complicated feat of freeing his arms, for he found himself minus his watch as well as his matches—plainly a refinement of cruelty on the part of The Parson. If his three companions, Burns, Thrale and Ellsworth, had been able to break into the house and search it, they must have done so much earlier, for it was presumably long after one o'clock. Even if they had actually been exploring the cellar while he was taking down and setting up the candle, Captain Vindex realized that he never would have heard them, so intent had all his senses been on the safe performance of that desperately precarious act.

His life was being measured by the inch in wax, and there were barely seven inches of it left. If he was to live he would have to do his own saving, and do it fast. There was only one way out, and that way was straight in among the rats. If the ancient sewer hadn't been blocked or broken down, it might still be open to the river. If it extended any distance into the river he would drown. But to drown was better than being eaten alive.

Captain Vindex took off his coat and filled it with an armament of broken brick. Then he pushed it into the opening, crawling after it, candle in hand. Moving onward into the four-foot sewer he shouted and began to bombard the shadowy swarm of vermin reluctantly retreating before the advance of candle-light and of so defiant an enemy.

He progressed like a monstrous worm, stretching out flat to shove his coatload of ammunition ahead of him, humping his body to come up with it, hurling his missiles and recovering them as he reached them. The rats, still numerous, kept a respectful distance, partly because of his occasional lucky shots.

Many hours had passed in this horrible pursuit of rats down a never-ending tunnel, or so it seemed to Captain Vindex, when he was startled by a distant rumble that rose to a thunderous roar. The ground shook under him. The candle, down to its last inch, fluttered perilously. Then, after minutes, the roar died back into the rumble and stopped suddenly. He realized that he had passed under the wide Drive, under the park below it, and had at last reached the railroad out on the bank of the Hudson. A freight train had been passing above him. He also realized that the crucial point of his underground journey was at hand. The sewer must be nearly at water level.

The rats appeared to know it too, for a few yards further on they refused to be driven and began to collect in a compact and menacing army, their fierce eyes gleaming closer to the already guttering candle-light. Captain Vindex rose to his torn and bleeding knees. Holding the light high and shading his eyes from it, he saw a liquid shimmer just beyond the restless battle array of the rats. With their backs to the water they were ready to attack upon his next advance.

Captain Vindex chose the initiative. Getting his feet under him he plunged desperately forward, half bent over. He trampled across the swarm of squealing vermin. Half covered with them he splashed into the water, bitten in a dozen places. But with water to his knees he dived, freeing himself of his tormentors, who hurriedly dropped their holds to swim back to safety.

When Captain Vindex came up he found the airspace in the sewer reduced to a few inches. It was live or die now, and with a vengeance. Filling his lungs to their utmost capacity with the bad air of the sewer, he plunged under again and swam desperately. Both head and chest were on the verge of bursting when he suddenly realized that he could see, though dimly. Light was penetrating the water. With a last prodigious effort he headed upward, and within three short but agonizing seconds he broke out into dawn-bright air.

He was less than ten yards from the shore of the river.

5

THE ONLY CLUE

"THE FACT THAT Cantwell knew the number on that bill plainly points to collusion with somebody in the bank," asserted Captain Vindex. "And that's the only clue we have left."

His three companions, returned to the penthouse from One Hundred and Fifteenth Street in no little anxiety after their futile search of the premises, had been amazed at his reappearance some hours later. They had been shocked and startled by the brief recital of his experience. Now, bathed, changed and mended, he again occupied his chair at the head of the mahogany table.

"I agree," said Thrale, the ex-lawyer, slowly. "But even if it were true I don't see how you, as Mr. Common Citizen George B. Arthur, without influence except as a depositor under that name, can force any evidence or acknowledgment of it. There's no suggestion of crime in a bank's noting down the number of any bill it passes out. And the mere institution of proceedings would involve complete publicity regarding the cause of them, including the kidnaping of Lora Perham."

"Meaning her death warrant if she hadn't already been returned or killed," nodded Captain Vindex. "And we have hours, not months, in which to act. No, what I propose to try at the bank is an immediate *coup de main*."

"A which?" asked Burns.

"You'll find out. You may take a principal part in it."

"How?"

"By impersonating an officer of the law, if necessary, to throw a scare into the cashier who gave me the bills. If there was anything crooked it might work. He looks like a fairly weak sister, and he was a little too apologetic about the short delay it took to get them for me."

"How's that? Were they new bills?"

"Yes, in packages."

"An' that's funny, too," frowned Burns. "I've got no badge, of course," he said slowly. "I turned it in when I resigned from the Division. What bank is it?"

"The National Commercial. It happens to be Perham's bank, too."

Steve Burns' face brightened with a momentary smile. "Did I tell you we nearly got pinched comin' out of that damn house up town, Captain Vindex? No? Well, the flatfoot on the beat heard us crash it, so he called out the reserves an' we walked right into 'em. As it happened, I knew the sergeant in charge, havin' once had official dealings with him—or, he knew me, rather. But he didn't know I'd quit the service. So I handed him a steer about the place bein' suspected as a hide-out for dope or something, told him we hadn't found a sign of it, an' he never even asked for a look at my badge. So he couldn't pin a thing on me in the way of impersonation. It was all his own idea. Well, then we just walked off. How's that?"

"It was lucky," said Captain Vindex. "But how does it fit?"

"Like an old shoe," said Burns. "Maybe! It so happens I know the Special down at the National Commercial the same way. Dixon. He's an old-timer. If he's still there—"

"He is," broke in Captain Vindex. "That settles it. At nine o'clock we'll be at the bank, but we've got an hour yet before we start. Kato's going to give us something to eat."

"Tell me, then," said Ellsworth. "You saw The Parson, Captain Vindex. How do you figure him?"

"As a fiend of the first water, to be exterminated as soon as possible and by any method," answered Captain Vindex slowly. "However little he may once have amounted to as Floyd Acton, he's found himself at last. His brother's murder did it. The taste of blood has turned him into a tiger. Yes, I saw him. But thanks to his mask and the highly exaggerated pose he adopted, I wouldn't know him if I met him in the street. I'm sure he's shrewd enough to mingle unsuspected with any average crowd; and is also able enough, owing to his intelligence and his ferocity, to control any sort of an army of gangsters."

"Sounds like a pretty tough citizen," said Burns. "Are you sure he wouldn't know you again, either?"

"That was his one mistake," said Captain Vindex. "He had me figured out like a book of logic. But he was so sure of rubbing me out that he didn't bother to strip me of my make-up. Apart from the rats, though, he knew the sewer from end to end, or thought he did. And as a matter of fact, there had been more of it. But something had caused the river to scour the bottom out from under it, and fifty feet of the pipe had recently broken off. Another two feet would have served to drown me."

"What?" stared Thrale. "How—"

Captain Vindex smiled grimly. "You can give the devil his due. After I got some air into my lungs I went down again to investigate. I'd learned enough respect for The Parson to doubt the possibility of his blundering, and I wanted to make sure."

"Good God!"

"So in the first place he must be convinced that I'm dead, and in the second place he isn't going to recognize me for a while. An active Captain Vindex is going to puzzle and alarm him—until he learns the truth."

Steve Burns looked at Captain Vindex with something like awe. "For all you got to say about this Parson and his brains an' all his works, Captain Vindex, I'll say I'm glad I'm stringing along with you!"

"Here comes Kato. Let's eat," said Captain Vindex.

6

KATO'S JUGGERNAUT

THE NATIONAL COMMERCIAL BANK had been open for business but five minutes when one of its good accounts appeared in the lobby accompanied by a big man with a face that looked as stiff as a mask, and who, though dressed in blue civilian serge, oozed a highly official air.

Special Officer Dixon bowed politely to the good account: "Morning, Mr. Arthur." Then his eyes went to the good account's companion and he smiled and held out a hand. "Hello, Brother Burns, long time no see. Got a hen on in this town?"

"Well, if isn't Flycop Dixon! Off the force and got you a nice cushy job, I see. What, me? Oh, nothing much. I just come here with Mr. Arthur on a little matter he's interested in—about some money he drew the other day. And say, old-timer, couldn't you just tip off the cashier so he'd answer us a simple question or two? He might want to freeze us."

Dixon's eyes widened. "What's up? Nothing about any queer stuff, is it? Not here in this bank?"

"Nothing like that," laughed Burns. "Something else entirely."

"Sure," said Officer Dixon, unbelieving. "You mean him in the A to E cage, Mr. Arthur? That's Norland."

Preceding them to the cage, the special officer put his face to the wicket and murmured a few words to the cashier. Then, with the reluctance of a natural curiosity, he left. The cashier stared at the two visitors with something like apprehension.

"Do you remember giving me five hundred the other day, Mr. Norland?" asked Captain Vindex without any preliminaries.

"Why—yes, I think I do, Mr. Arthur," answered the cashier nervously, flicking his eyes toward Burns. "Last Thursday—all in tens and twenties, wasn't it? Was anything wrong?"

"Only that somebody in the bank must have taken the numbers of the bills. Why?"

"I don't know. I mean I don't know anything about it, Mr. Arthur. Why, I haven't the slightest idea what the numbers were."

"Nor I," said Captain Vindex dryly. "But someone did."

"Excuse me, Mr. Arthur," said Burns, "let me handle it." He looked swiftly over the floor. Owing to the early hour only a few other customers were present, and none were near. Burns leaned in toward Norland. "Listen, young man," he said in a low but impressive voice, "there's all kinds of funny business mixed up with this thing. Better come across. Not with what you *don't* know, but with what you *do!* Now how about it? No stalling!"

"I—I didn't take the numbers myself and I don't know that anybody did," said the cashier, uncomfortable under the cold blue eyes boring into him. "Or why anyone should have, though—"

"Though *what?*"

"Well, I remember that when I sent for the bills—you see the noon rush had almost cleaned me out of cash for the moment—I was told that—that one of the officers wanted to see them first."

"Who was it?"

"Mr. Fall—the president, Mr. Simeon Fall. We've found a few counterfeits lately, and he probably—"

"Back up! New money fresh from the Federal Reserve, wasn't it? Well then?"

"Yes, that's so." Cashier Norland shook his head helplessly. "Then I don't see—"

"I guess you don't. You wouldn't."

STEVE BURNS AND Captain Vindex looked at each other. Then they stepped aside to one of the marble writing stands.

"Acts as though Dixon had tipped him off I was the whole Secret Service," frowned Burns. "Anyway, it worked. But why the hell would the president of a bank like this want to give the once over to a small bunch of money paid out to a known depositor? I can't seem to make sense out of it. Now if it had been to some well known crook, an' the police—"

"Wait a minute!" broke in Captain Vindex. "I've got one more question." He led the way back to the cashier's cage. "Tell me, Mr. Norland, have you any account here under the name of Acton—Floyd Acton?"

Norland flushed. "Sorry, Mr. Arthur, but we're not supposed—" his eye caught Burns' hand on its way up to the lapel of his coat, or toward what might lie beneath it. "No, sir," he shifted, responsive to the suggestive gesture. "We have no account under the name of Floyd Acton." There seemed to be a note of relief in his tone.

But Burns thought he caught something else in it.

"Or any other Acton?" he asked.

The cashier hesitated. "Well—a Mr. Reuben Acton."

"Reuben, huh?" Burns frowned at him. "And would he happen to have been in here the same day Mr. Arthur was? Do you remember?"

"No, I don't know. I can't remember," said the hapless cashier, mopping his forehead. "He might have been. But look here, gentlemen, what's this all about? I'm likely to get into trouble for discussing the bank's business. Mr. Fall's very strict about such matters. Why not go to Mr. Fall himself for information?"

"Is he in?"

"No, not yet."

"Maybe we will," said Burns. "If we do we won't mention having talked to you, if you like. Provided you keep your own trap shut! How about it?"

Norland smiled feebly. "That suits me. I won't breathe it."

"O.K. Then I'll tip Dixon off too, though he don't know a thing anyway."

ON THEIR WAY out Burns consulted New York's ten or more telephone directories. At the door he farewelled Dixon with a finger held impressively to his lips. The special officer looked wise and wagged complete understanding. Not until they were in a taxi did either Burns or Captain Vindex speak.

"Well, and what does Mr. George B. Arthur think of that?"

"Reuben Acton isn't necessarily a unique name. There might be several of them," replied Captain Vindex.

"There might be. But there ain't a single one, not in Manhattan nor even in Brooklyn, Long Island, or the Bronx. That don't mean much. If he's got one he wouldn't have it listed. It only goes to show there's no other Reuben Actons to mix him up with. Most honest men with bank accounts are in the telephone book."

Captain Vindex smiled queerly. "You feel pretty sure that the bank's Reuben Acton is The Parson."

"I got a hunch—no, I'm putting two an' two together. Listen. There was your five hundred. Foxie Gordon got it an' then he got his. Why? Because Cantwell, who was The Parson's man, recognized the numbers. And Floyd Acton, who you say doubles for his dead brother, Reuben Acton, is The Parson. That adds up to what?"

"Two and two make four."

"Yeah. *But!* Where does Mr. Bank President Fall fit into the addition? Seems to me he almost makes it sound like two an' two make five, or I'm no mathematician."

"If you're not, I'm not," admitted Captain Vindex. "In any case, we've got to take a chance. I'm thinking of a shot in the dark at Mr. Fall that might bring him down. In that event it's possible that we'd have another clue to Lora Perham."

"My God, yes, the kid!" gritted Burns. "They might saw another finger off her!"

"That was for my benefit," said Captain Vindex. "Now that I've been safely disposed of I doubt if The Parson will harm her further, for the time being, at least. Nevertheless, we have to act without delay."

Burns was staring pointedly ahead.

"Yeah, you're dead—for the time being," he said grimly. "But how about a guy named George Arthur, who drew out the kale that got Foxie Gordon killed an' then Cantwell an' then you—for the time being? Would he be likely to get into trouble like the rest, considering that the numbers of them bills seem to have got spotted all along the line?"

"He might and then again he mightn't. Why?"

"*Might* comes nearer. Take a look over our man's shoulder into the rear view mirror. See what I mean? I don't like it."

"You mean the big closed job that's been following us for the past few blocks?" inquired Captain Vindex calmly. "Take a look at the truck just to one side of it and a little behind."

"The one with the Jap driving it? My God, it's Kato!" exclaimed Burns. "You mean to say he's trailing us in that thing?"

"Kato's pet juggernaut," Captain Vindex smiled. "You'll see it in action if the sedan makes a suspicious move. Yes, he's practically been on our heels ever since we started for the bank. Looking after me is a habit of his, and Kato has a most uncanny instinct for things that are going to happen."

"Well," breathed out Burns heavily, "I'll say it's a damn good— *Look out!*"

The truck, which had been crowding the sedan a little, swung left toward the middle of Broadway. The man at the wheel of the sedan, seeing a clear road ahead, stepped hard on the gas in order to pass the taxi at close quarters. From the rear window of the taxi Burns saw one of the pair in the back seat of the black car lift a machine gun and rest its muzzle on the edge of the open window of the sedan. His heart flew into his mouth.

But the truck, as if its driver sensed exactly what was happening, instantly swung right again at high speed, smashing almost head on into the sedan. Mingled with the crash of splintering wood and the clang of twisting steel there came a coughing rattle from the tommy. The man holding it had had his finger already on the trigger.

Their frightened taxi driver jammed a foot down on his own accelerator, and the last Steve Burns saw of the disaster was the vision of Kato leaping down from the high seat of the truck to disappear among the gathering crowd. The shattered sedan lay on its side. Burns looked at Captain Vindex in some amazement.

"Don't you even stop an' pick him up when he jumps off the dock?" he asked as soon as he could speak.

"Kato'll turn up smiling, truck and all, after the cops have gone over the ruins. A carload of smashed-up gangsters will interest them much more than a runaway truck driver."

Burns was silent for a few moments. Then: "You gave The Parson a fair recommendation as a good fast worker and all, when you got back this morning, Captain Vindex. But it looks to me as if you hadn't told the half of it. Damned if he isn't on the job *all* the time! What do we do next to give his nasty disposition some target practice?"

"I'm going to get in touch with Perham. He's the man to fire that shot in the dark at President Simeon Fall of the National Commercial."

7

THE SNARE

AN ANGULAR GIRL in black, wearing spectacles and with her hair drawn tightly back from her bulging forehead, slipped into the private office of the President with a hush-hush air of high efficiency.

"Mr. Walter Perham on the wire, Mr. Fall. He wishes to speak to you personally. Shall I put him on your special line?"

"Walter Perham? One of our largest depositors, Miss Brenner," said the big man solemnly. "He should always have access. Yes, put him on my line."

The secretary slipped out, closing the door as noiselessly as she had opened it. The banker waited, his eyes fixed with a curious expression of expectancy on his gold and ivory desk set. It tinkled. He raised the receiver to his ear.

"Mr. Perham? Ah, good morning, Mr. Perham… What's that?… Yes, Mr. Perham, absolutely. No one can possibly listen in from this end. This is my private wire."

For the next ten seconds a cynical smile twitched at Fall's lips. But when he answered he adapted the expression of his face to the tenor of his words. He frowned seriously and majestically.

"One hundred thousand dollars in cash? But isn't that

rather extraordinary, Mr. Perham, even for a man of your... Yes, yes, I know, but the bank—"

The smile flickered again across the face of Mr. Fall. Then he cleared his throat audibly in front of the telephone. "You'll pardon me, my dear Mr. Perham, but your agitation sounds almost alarming. I trust no serious crisis in your business affairs is... oh, no, no! If you say it's a purely personal matter it's so, of course. But still... what? Yes, no doubt the securities would amply cover any deficiencies in the account, but... Well, I'll say yes. Your credit—"

He drew out his watch as he listened. "Fifteen minutes? It will take about that time to get the amount together in small bills, Mr. Perham, but it will be ready... Not coming yourself?... I see," he said slowly "That would be at your own risk of course, Mr. Perham... I shall expect him then. Good-by."

He laid up the phone and pushed a button on his desk. The secretary reappeared like a noiseless cuckoo out of a noiseless clock.

"Yes, Mr. Fall?"

"Tell Jones to bring me one hundred thousand dollars in old bills in a satchel, Miss Brenner. Nothing larger than twenties and fifties. Mr. Perham is sending for it, and when his messenger arrives have him come in to me. Ask them to send me also a statement of Perham's account."

"Yes, Mr. Fall."

"Oh, and at the same time they might as well let me have an Acton statement. Reuben Acton."

"Yes, Mr. Fall."

TEN MINUTES LATER both statements were on his desk

and the satchel full of money stood on the floor beside it. In another five minutes Miss Brenner re-opened the door.

"Mr. Perham's messenger is here, Mr. Fall."

"Send him in."

The President of the National Commercial Bank of New York looked sharply at the messenger as the door closed behind him. Fall had expected to see a man who could naturally be taken for one of Perham's trusted employes, or a man of the type to be hired for his wits, muscle and fidelity, from any of the public protective agencies. The man who entered suggested neither. He wore good clothes too well and, except for the peculiar set expression of his face and eyes, might have been a typical member of any high-class club. Yet the banker knew he had never seen him before.

"You come from Mr. Perham?" asked Fall.

"I've brought you a note from him," said the messenger. He handed over the note. Fall opened it and read it.

"Why," frowned the banker, "he says he also gave you some sort of a token to show me in order that there could be no mistake. A rather romantic idea, considering that I know both his voice and his handwriting. However— what is it?"

"This," said the other man, offering him a small package.

Still frowning, Fall took it and undid it. The package contained an oblong leather box about four inches in length and of a type made to hold a small piece of jewelry. He dropped the box on the desk in front of him. "What's that?" he asked contemptuously. "Am I supposed to recognize some pet gewgaw that Perham wears in order to assure me that you come from no one else? What nonsense?"

"Nevertheless, a good deal depends on your recognizing it, Mr. Fall," he was surprised to be told, "and you're quite right—it's a pet gewgaw which Mr. Perham valued very highly."

The banker stared suspiciously, but after a slight hesitation he touched a finger to the spring. The cover flew up. Out of the box a thick ringlet of yellow hair crawled over its edge on to the desk. Within the box remained a little severed finger wearing a thin circle of gold.

The blood drained out of Simeon Fall's face till his cheeks looked like raw tripe. His lower jaw sagged and began to tremble. But he was unable to remove his fascinated gaze from the dreadful thing in the box.

"Is the token satisfactory, Mr. Fall?" inquired the messenger. "Sufficient warrant for handing over the money?"

Sick and faint, the banker covered his eyes with his hands. "Yes," he gasped, "take it—the bag down there on the floor. And take away—this thing!"

"The finger? But why not keep it as a souvenir! Or as some justification for turning over a hundred thousand dollars of the bank's money solely on the strength of a telephone conversation, without even a line in writing to show for it. As you must have seen, the note contains not one direct word about the money."

SIMEON FALL WAS no fool. There was a gun in a drawer of his desk. Under the edge of the desk were a dozen buttons, by pressing any of which he could summon attendance or assistance. But in view of the instructions he had given, and especially in view of the thing that lay on the desk, there was no explanation he could make which might not involve far-reaching consequences. And he feared that under the unexpected shock of seeing the child's amputated finger he had betrayed himself. But to *whom?*

His hands dropped and anxiety stared out of his eyes. Panic rose to choke him. He had to swallow several times before he could speak.

"Do—do you really come from Perham?" he croaked hoarsely. Then a faint gleam of hope tricked him. "Or did—were you sent by—do you know whom I mean?" Instantly he knew he had said too much.

"You mean Reuben Acton—The Parson," shot back the other man, "No, I represent neither of them. That is, I did come with a note from Walter Perham, but like his telephone message, it was dictated by me. And the gewgaw in the box is a reminder from The Parson, as you so manifestly guessed. As for me, let us say, Mr. Fall, that I came from God—or from the Devil if you prefer—to put the finger on you. I seem to have succeeded."

The banker sat back in his chair, his face sweating, his portly body flaccid and inert. Captain Vindex shook him back into consciousness.

"So *you* were The Peddler, the cowardly fiend in the background, who sold Lora Perham," said Captain Vindex softly. "I had suspected it, but you yourself have confessed it as if in so many words! So this is your work!" He picked the little white finger out of its casket and thrust it in the banker's face.

Fall cracked completely. "Oh, my God!" he moaned. "But how could I know—how could I dream he'd do anything like that! I never would have had anything to do with it if—if—"

Captain Vindex peered down at the two statements

lying on the desk. "And you were already figuring your own profits from the snatch! Practically a transfer from one account to the other, except for your own filthy commission," he said grimly. "Look!" he commanded, pointing to successive large deposits listed on the Acton sheet. "What does *that* represent? And *that*? And *that*? Was that ransom money, too? More blood money?"

"Not—not blood money," Fall gasped out. "No one was ever injured—before. They all—paid!"

"And you got yours?"

"Listen! I beg you to listen!" the banker suddenly broke out, spurred to sudden desperation. "I couldn't help myself! I'd lost—I'd borrowed too much money, and I'd—mixed up some accounts. It was after the crash—after I'd held on just as long as I could! Then—*he* came. He knew! God, can't you see how it happened? When he asked me who was still rich, who still had plenty of ready money, I— I—"

"Sold out your friends, your customers, your depositors. You peddled their money or their lives or their children to The Parson; knowing, thanks to your position, just how much each of them would be worth to a kidnaper—and collected your twenty per cent of blood and tears and horror!" Captain Vindex struck the banker a heavy blow in the face. "Tell me! Where's The Parson now? You must know—you must communicate with him."

FALL CRINGED, MORE at the question than at the blow. "I—I don't—" Captain Vindex raised his hand again.

"Don't!" mumbled the banker. "You—you hurt me! I'll tell. He's at a place up in the mountains—the Catskills—a little hunting lodge of mine that he—he took possession of. You've broken my face!"

"Go and clean it up," commanded Captain Vindex. "We're going to call on The Parson!"

Fall quailed. "He'll kill me!"

"Then he'll have to beat me to it. Come!"

Captain Vindex stood over Fall, even assisted him while he made his injured features more presentable. "Now we're going out through the bank," he told him. "If you create the least suspicion that you're not going willingly I'll kill you and announce your complicity in the kidnaping of Lora Perham then and there. If you have to, you can explain that you're accompanying me to Perham's office with the money. Otherwise, if you care for a few more hours of life, you'll come quietly."

Despite the strange transformation in Simeon Fall's customary appearance of importance and authority, no one ventured to accost him on the way out. In the lobby a big man engaged in conversation with Special Officer Dixon glanced at them, broke off his conversation, and fell into step at the banker's vacant side without a word. At the curb a uniformed Japanese chauffeur sprang out of a purring limousine to open the door for them, while behind the limousine waited another car, a high-powered runabout, occupied by two men.

Not until both cars were well on to the Washington Bridge did Fall's captors relax their intense guard.

"President Simeon Fall of the National Commercial kidnaped right out of his own bank in broad daylight!" said Steve Burns suddenly. "If that isn't beating The Parson at his own game I'll be double-damned. So you had the right dope on him after all!"

"It was the shot in the dark I had poor Perham fire that put the finger on him," said Captain Vindex.

Simeon Fall, between them, groaned like a lost soul. Then he, too, spoke. Not to his companions but to himself, staring blankly into space as if he were utterly alone, his whole world fallen away from him.

"The devil!" he muttered in a tone of dull bewilderment. "The liar, the shameless and unscrupulous liar! And he solemnly promised me on his honor, he swore by all that was holy that nothing should ever be known about our connection, that nothing could ever touch me! Oh, God punish him! God punish him!"

8

THE HOUSE GREED BUILT

FLOYD ACTON, *ALIAS* Reuben Acton, *alias* The Parson, lay comfortably extended in a lounging chair on the veranda of what Mr. Fall liked to refer to as his "little hunting lodge in the Catskills." The sun was already dropping behind the rampart of Mt. Ashland, a mile to west.

The Parson had returned to the lodge just as the sun was rising that morning, had slept long and soundly in the consciousness of a night well spent in New York, had breakfasted hours after lunch time. He was now relaxing with a bottle beside him, considering the replacement of Cantwell and how to proceed with a program no longer subject to embarrassment by an obtrusive Captain Vindex.

Fall's little hunting lodge, isolated not only by its situation but also by a high steel fence surrounding his twenty acres of estate, contained all the comforts of home except electricity. Nor was The Parson neglecting a like easement of the rigors of life during his temporary appropriation of Mr. Fall's rustic hide-out. He set down his glass and raised his voice.

"Mag!"

Finally the sound of heels clicking on the oak stairway came through the open door. But instead of approaching from the hall to the veranda they turned into the living room. A mild glow in a window announced the lighting of a lamp inside.

"Mag!" barked The Parson again with ominous vigor, but without turning his head. The steps clicked out to the stand beside him.

"I'm here," said the girl sullenly. "Wouldn't you even gimme time to light the lamp? And for God's sake, haven't I ast you not to Mag me? My name's Madge!"

The Parson looked at her, his eyes expressionless. Her hair was a straggled blaze of peroxide. Diamonds glittered in her ears, at her throat and on her fingers, yet her purple satin negligée was spotted and wrinkled. Her cheeks showed a high color of their own, though of a different red from that with which they were touched up.

"Me too," said The Parson coldly. "But that's what you look like—just plain *Mag*."

"Well, who wouldn't?" blazed the girl. "With all I got to do, besides stickin' round this last end of nowhere an' nobody even to talk to!"

"You're talking to *me now*. And forgetting that 'It is better to dwell in a corner of the housetop, than with a brawling woman in a wide house'—see Proverbs Twenty-One, Nine."

MADGE'S FACE PALED underneath the rouge.

"Don't," she said, forcing a smile. "You know you scare the daylights out of me when you begin slingin' the Bible at me, honey. I didn't mean a thing."

"Then why don't you come when I call? Where were you?"

A little courage showed again in her cheeks. "Where

would I be? Up stairs, o' course, tending to that damned whining little brat!"

"Be charitable, Madge, be charitable," purred The Parson. "Little Lora grieves at her unfortunate separation from her parents—and possibly also at her separation from her finger. No child of her age can be expected to show a proper spirit of resignation. Let us hope that she may soon be restored to her home."

"My God, aren't you a devil!" whispered the girl under her breath. The Parson smiled at the compliment. "Well, ain't it a sure thing?" she asked. "Ain't it time for Canty to get busy on the wire? You said this Perham had oodles of jack an' was the kind that would break his neck to come across with it."

"About Cantwell, now," chuckled The Parson. "I'm afraid that there's no telephone connection from hell, my dear Madge. No."

"What?" she stared. "You mean he's—"

"Yes. Cantwell apparently put his foot in it and slipped. I sent him on a necessary errand, and—no more Cantwell."

Madge was frightened. "Oh, my God! They got on to him? On to *us*? Listen, aren't we going to beat it, then? Please honey, don't be foolish! If they should ever spot this joint—"

"Shut up, fool!" snapped The Parson. "Cantwell got his, but it was one man gave it to him. That man has already been attended to. Don't you know me, yet? And this place is as safe as hell itself."

"You got him?"

"I got him."

Madge sat down shakily and reached for the bottle.

"And I nearly got heart disease," she tried to smile. "I need a drink."

The Parson slapped her hand away. "No. You've had plenty and you show it. Besides, you're going for a ride."

The girl's heart stopped beating for a second. Then she let her breath out. "Gee, how you do love to scare me, handsome!"

The Parson smiled. He did enjoy it. "Only into the big town this time, Madge. You're going to substitute for Cantwell and put in the first call to our friend Perham. From a dial phone some place where there are plenty of booths! Make it the Grand Central. I'll write out the message—exactly what you are to say and no more, understand? Then you hang up!"

Madge jumped. "Gee," she brightened, "into town! I feel like I hadn't seen a bright light for years an' years! Sure I understand, honey. Wait till I get dolled up!"

"*You* wait!" said The Parson softly. "Think you're going to get a chance to play round town and get stewed, you damned little fool? You're wrong. Rick drives you in, sees you to the booth, puts you back in the car and drives you right out here again!"

"But—but," she stammered, disappointed, "why, it'll take all night! If it's only to phone the sucker what's the sense of going way into New York? What's the matter with going down to that hick town by the river an' doing it from there? Damn!"

The Parson looked at her with cold contempt.

" 'Last of all the woman died also,'" he quoted. "See Luke Twenty, Verse Thirty-Two and take heed thereby. And you'll doll yourself *down*, not up! Take off all those rocks, wash your face clean and put on the plainest clothes you've got, you hear me? So that no one can remember seeing you, even. How about the child?"

"I—I give her some medicine," said Madge, altogether cowed. "She'll sleep all right till I get back."

"Doped her, did you? Well, if she dies it's *your* funeral."

"She's all right," said the girl hastily. "It can't hurt her. I'll go an' dress." She was turning when The Parson checked her.

"Wait! Somebody coming!"

A topless runabout, emerging from the distant trees, was slowly moving up the rough road toward the circle in front of the veranda. Madge held her breath while The Parson frowned and stared, slipping a hand under his coat.

"Only one man," he muttered. "But who was on the gate—Johnny? Next gate he sees he goes through himself, for good!"

The car was still some hundred yards away, and the growing twilight made it difficult to distinguish the features of the man who was driving it.

"Where are the other boys?" asked The Parson without moving his eyes or his lips. "Out back? Go get them, but keep them out of sight inside the house. No, hold on—by God, it's Fall!"

It was. Stopping the car in front of the veranda steps the banker climbed out of it, holding a black satchel ostentatiously in one hand and trying to paint an ingratiating smile on his sickly face.

9

THE TRAP IS SPRUNG

MR. FALL HAD been compelled to give road directions after his captors had turned inland at Catskill. A dozen miles up the Creek he had indicated a narrow dirt road winding westward as the one that led to the gate of his property, admitting that the lodge itself stood a quarter of a mile further inside the gate.

Ordered out of the limousine and expecting instant death, he had been astonished to have Captain Vindex transfer him to the runabout as its sole occupant, at the same time handing him the satchel full of money.

"Drive ahead," Captain Vindex had commanded. "If there's a man on guard at the gate who knows you he may let you in if you say you're bringing the ransom to The Parson. We can't afford to be stopped there."

Fall had obeyed. At the gate he had been challenged by an evil-looking man with an automatic and had hurriedly identified himself, showing the satchel of money in corroboration of his errand. The Parson's punk, his eyes sticking out, had opened the gate to let the banker through.

"Boy," he grinned, "I guess that buys you in, feller. The boss wouldn't want *that* kep' out!"

Those had been his last words. As the car began to

move on, a man had dropped from his concealment at its rear, ducked under the gun of the startled gate guard and smashed the butt of his own down on his skull. Fall had seen him die, and it had been too much for his delicate nerves. But Captain Vindex had turned on him fiercely.

"Pull yourself together and get going! Drive up to the lodge and offer to ransom Lora Perham with the hundred grand you have there in the bag! Try to get hold of her and bring her back here. We'll wait—for a time! It's up to you. If The Parson saw *us* coming he might kill her. And if I were you," Captain Vindex had warned him significantly, "I'd make every effort to persuade him and to quiet any suspicion he may have. It will be your brains or your life, I promise you!"

Fall had driven on mechanically, his mind clearing as he thought he saw his one chance in a hundred. He began to appreciate Captain Vindex's strategy. After all, it was the money that Reuben Acton was after, and a hundred thousand was the sum they had secretly decided on as an obtainable ransom for Lora Perham. While if he could rescue the child and give her into the hands of this devil whom he now knew to be called Captain Vindex, the latter might relent at least to the extent of letting him go alive. And Fall had also become convinced that if The Parson suspected any connection between him and those terrible avengers, even that he was merely their helpless victim, he would kill him on the spot.

So when the banker stepped out of the car it was with a most desperate hope and intention of putting the trick over. But his welcome was inauspicious.

"What in hell are you doing here?" The Parson

demanded viciously. "I throught we were to have no contact with each other except on ordinary business at the bank!"

FALL'S EYE FELL on Madge, staring at him from the doorway, and he colored with embarrassment.

"Can't a man visit his own property and call on his tenant?" he tried to say lightly.

"No!" snapped The Parson. "I want nobody coming here and I expect nobody, and you know why—especially a damned old fool like you, who wouldn't know he was being followed if they stepped all over his heels! How'd you get by the gate?"

Fall paled at the recollection of what had happened at the gate. "I—why, the man let me in," he said lamely. "Why not?"

"He'll never let anybody else in!" threatened The Parson.

Fall looked sicker. Acton didn't know how right he was.

"But I—I wanted to see you," said the banker. "I've brought you something." He glanced again at the girl with plain significance.

"Spit it out," said The Parson. "She's all right, she's in on it. And she knows who *you* are! What do you mean, you brought us something?"

Fall crimsoned with a new humiliation. Did *everybody* know he was connected with a kidnaper? Also, his terror increased. The warm summer day seemed to be turning very cold.

"It's this," he stammered, holding out the satchel. "The— the ransom."

"The *what?*" Seizing the satchel, The Parson opened it and took note of the contents, apparently without losing sight for a moment of the man who had brought it. "How'd

you get hold of this—ransom money?" he asked in a voice
that sounded to Fall like the whir of a rattlesnake hidden
in the bushes.

"Why," stuttered the banker, "I—he—Perham called me
up this morning and—and asked me to fix it for him—get
the money together for him, I mean. And then I thought,"
he blundered on, "that perhaps the best thing I could do
was to bring it myself and end the thing at once—get the
child back to him. So—so if you'll let me have her—"

The Parson laughed in his face.

"By God, you *are* a fool! Listen," he said with sudden
softness, "did you tell him he could have the kid back for
a hundred grand?"

Simeon Fall was shocked white.

"Of course not!" he gasped. "Do you think I'm insane?
Do you dream I'd commit myself in any such way? Of
course not! I'm—I was utterly ignorant of the affair!"

The Parson's eyes glittered. "Ah? Then why did Perham
apply to *you* about the money?"

Fall stared at him. "Why? Because he needed it—
because I'm his banker—because you'd demanded it of
him, I suppose?"

"But I hadn't," smiled The Parson. "I haven't even
broached the subject of ransom to him—yet! So what?"

So nothing, as far as Simeon Fall was concerned. He
didn't know the answer. But he did realize that something
had gone wrong, that his mind was dizzy and that he was
sick with fear. He stood like a stump.

"I'll tell you," said The Parson smoothly. "You lost your
nerve completely and decided to get out of it as quick as
you could. But you knew I wouldn't stand for losing all that

kale—or any of it! So you took your own money—or the bank's," he suggested dryly, "and actually thought you could take the child away from me and do me out of a hundred thousand dollars. Isn't that it?"

Fall gaped.

"Do you—out of a hundred thousand dollars?" he repeated dumbly, "But—but there it is! You've got it!"

THE PARSON GRINNED all over his face. "But not *Perham's* hundred grand! Yours is accepted with thanks. You won't need it any more, anyway. But I intend to get Perham's too, and I hold the kid until I do. Then I'll have *two* hundred grand. You see?"

"I—don't understand," faltered the dazed banker.

The Parson's features suddenly straightened to their most unctuous and pietistic phase. He shook his head sadly. "Woe to them that will not understand! For the Good Book says, 'Answer a fool according to his folly, lest he be wise in his own conceit,'—see Proverbs Twenty-Six, Five,—*and here's my answer!*" He shot his right hand forward, the sleeve-gun leaping into it. Instantly there was a roar of flame and smoke, and a heavy slug from the derringer tore through Simeon Fall's aldermanic belly. The banker dropped writhing and shrieking to the floor of the veranda.

Madge stared white from the doorway, her hands at her mouth.

"The bloody skunk!" said The Parson correctly. "Lie to me, would he? Try to break away from me, would he? Well, he got what was coming to him." Fixing a foot under Fall's flopping body, he heaved it down the steps into the driveway. Then he looked after it frowning. "Something happened," The Parson decided. "No man sitting as pretty as he was would have made a move like that unless he was pushed!"

But the loud shot was followed by further consequences than the mere killing of Simeon Fall. The Parson's other henchmen, three in all, who had been in the back of the house, came running to the front to post themselves, guns out, behind the frozen woman in the doorway.

The Parson turned and scowled from the top of the veranda steps. "Nothing for you punks to do. Put up your gats. I just rubbed out a rat, that's all. Donovan, you and Smoky go find a spade to pat him in the face with. Dig a hole in the garden behind the house. No, dig two holes," he bethought himself, "or make a double bed! Rick, you go down to the gate and chase Johnny up here if you can find him. I want him!"

They were moving to obey when there came a stuttering like that of a tommy from the direction of the gate. A second car careened round the curve among the trees, to pound up the road toward the lodge, its cut-out wide open. A limousine. The Parson gave it an astounded glance, then his face turned into a mask of fury. With a bound he cleared the steps to the earth, where he emptied his gun into Simeon Fall's still twitching body.

His punks at the door shouted at him and began firing recklessly over his head, then past him as he dashed back up the steps. For lead was already flying from the limousine as it commenced to brake to a stop, spraying dust and gravel, thirty feet behind the runabout that had brought the banker. But The Parson reached the door untouched, slamming the oaken barrier after him as he crossed the threshold.

"The lousy rat!" gasped The Parson. "So that was the heat in his double-cross, only I got him too quick!" He peeked through a curtained sidelight. "Five of them and they're spreading," he barked. "Get to the windows, you!"

Madge cowered at the foot of the stairs. The Parson glared at her. "Maybe they've got us! All they got to do is burn or freeze us out—and that means you too! But I'll be eternally damned if they get Lora Perham besides! Get up stairs and finish her off, you sick doll! Show your stuff— stick her or strangle her! *Go!*"

Shots already crackled in the rooms at each side of the hall and there was a sudden crash of glass.

10

V FOR VENGEANCE

DEATH HAD HER cornered, and Madge kindled with the savage rancor of despair. She rose and raced up the stairs and into the back room where Lora Perham had been held a hidden captive for nearly a week. Thanks to the opiate, the child was heavily asleep as Madge had told The Parson she would be. She lay on a cot at the side of the room, her tangled yellow curls like a halo on the pillow. A little bandaged hand hung over the edge of the cot.

The woman stood over her and stared down at her. Then with a practiced movement she lifted the purple negligée and snatched a small thin knife from her garter. She raised the blade.

At that instant a hand was clamped around her throat and she was seized by the hair from behind. The knife clattered to the floor. Madge's head was drawn back against the fulcrum of the grip on her throat until she would have been staring at the ceiling—except that she found herself staring into an Oriental face covered with a broad smile. Out of that face two narrow eyes were looking at her with the fierceness of a tiger. She tried to scream, but she could emit only a weak squeak. Her head was drawn back still further. Then there was a dull snap like the breaking of a stick.

Kato dropped the body and cat-footed out into the hall to listen at the head of the stairs. Battle was still rattling below, but a cloud of smoke that was more than gunsmoke was pouring out of the lower room on the left and beginning to drift up the stairway. He shook his head and went back into the bedroom, where his eyes flicked from the child asleep on the cot to the woman dead on the floor.

Suddenly he picked up Madge's body; moving to the window by which he had entered, he flung it unconcernedly through the window to the ground outside. Then he stepped to the cot and picked up the child, wrapping her tenderly in a blanket while he murmured shrill small words of Japanese endearment into her unhearing ears. Holding her little figure carefully to one arm, he went again to the window and slipped over the sill.

DOWNSTAIRS, IN A room thick with smoke, the battle was coming to an end: Captain Vindex had turned it into a fight at close quarters almost at the very beginning, by hurling himself through a window from the veranda into the living room. In the fall which saved him from the quick shot fired at him he had brought down the table with the lighted lamp. The lamp broke and the spilled oil caught, the flames spreading rapidly to the flimsy summer furnishings and draperies of the room. The thickening smoke soon made it possible for the rest of the attackers to get inside the house, and the disconcerted gangsters were pressed back into the hall and the already blazing living room.

All at once the shooting ceased. After a few seconds of silence Steve Burns cautiously raised himself from behind a sofa in the corner and peered through running eyes into the whirling smoke.

"It's me," he ventured. "Who's here an' how's it coming?"

"All right, I think," coughed Thrale from somewhere. "The doctor's over this side, and we've left one lying in the hall. There are two others down in this room, maybe more."

Somebody stepped out in the half-light of the flames that rose from the floor and crackled up the wall.

"Drag them out, then," he snapped.

"We've got to see—"

"Look out!" shouted Burns, as he jerked up his gun and pulled, only to have the pin click on an empty shell. "Behind you! Captain Vindex!"

A man with a mask stepped out of a shroud of smoke and fired even as Burns was crying out. But his hand faltered for a split second at the shouted name, and the shot went wild. "You!" he spat. "Damn you, how in hell—" He fired again and missed again in the dancing smoke. Then, just as Captain Vindex started to turn, the masked man flung the gun straight at his head; instantly he darted back into the smoke and crashed through a window out on to the veranda.

"It's The Parson!"

Captain Vindex's voice was electrifying. All four men plunged blindly out of the house by the door and by the windows. But as they cleared their eyes on the veranda the starter of the runabout began to grind. Recklessly they ran toward it, shooting, and the shooting was returned. Yet, strangely, not one of them was hit. Then the runabout lurched and leaped and was off with a roar into the gathering darkness.

CAPTAIN VINDEX WAS the first to wheel toward the limousine. But he stopped before he reached it. Its front tires were wheezing their last—they were already practically flat.

"That's why he hit nobody," he said grimly. "He was making sure of no pursuit."

Far down the winding road the tail light of the runabout winked mockingly back at him before it disappeared behind the black screen of trees.

Captain Vindex shrugged his shoulders and turned toward the lodge. "All in to look for Lora Perham! In fifteen minutes the place will be filled with smoke!"

But Kato appeared from the corner of the veranda with a bundle in his arms.

"Have got little small child," he announced. "And lady lying very dead behind house. Get neck broken and fall through window because wish to stick knife in child. I stop."

"Hell's bells!" said Steve Burns softly. "Hell's—*bells!*"

Dr. Ellsworth took Lora Perham and squatted down in the roadway, while someone switched on the lights of the limousine.

Captain Vindex drew a long breath. "Well, it's all over but the mopping up. Drag Fall over here—and somebody help me get out the three in the house. That will make four of them."

"Don't forget lady behind house," said Kato. "She try to stick knife in little small child."

"Five," said Captain Vindex.

"Six," said Kato, "I go get man down by gate, then I put on spare wheels."

"Yes. How is she, Doctor?"

"Pulse is all right. She's been doped, but not dangerously. Rather a good thing under the circumstances. And the hand isn't infected. She'll live."

"Oh, good!" said Kato. Then he turned again to Captain Vindex. "Seven are right number. You find seven in trunk back of car. I go now."

Burns stared at him as he trotted away. Then he went to the rear of the limousine and unstrapped the trunk to look into it. "My God!" he said. "That's what I call efficiency! What do you s'pose is in the trunk? Acton! I mean Cantwell!"

"It's not Kato's fault we can't make it eight," said Captain Vindex grimly.

Twenty minutes later the seven corpses were laid out in a row in the middle of the grass plot around which the road circled. The low roof of the house was beginning to fall in. Captain Vindex took something like a lighter from his pocket, held it until it glowed red, and then bent over the still figures, one by one. When he stepped away from them the little box containing Lora Perham's accusing finger lay on Simeon Fall's breast, while the rising moon was silvering the seven white foreheads except where a thin red V was lightly burned into the center of each.

"The sign of the Avenger—the seal of a bloody retribution!" said Dr. Ellsworth in a low awed voice.

"Just that," said Captain Vindex. "And The Parson will surely hear of it, even if as yet he's missed seeing it or wearing it; for the burning of Simeon Fall's hunting lodge will bring the State police here before morning. Something for him to think about when we meet with him again!"

"Car are all fix," said Kato. "Now can take little small child back safe to home."

THE BRAND OF VINDEX

The Go-Between Who Says He Will Rescue the Kidnaped Woman Is the Fiend Who Holds Her Prisoner—the Fiend That Vindex and the Five Avengers Know as The Parson

1

THE DEVIL'S GO-BETWEEN

THE ROOM WAS a library partly walled with books set in recessed niches and interspaced with panels of rich English walnut. The house stood two hundred feet from the street at the loop of a winding driveway, deep in its wide acre of lawn dotted with trees, shrubs and fancy flower pots. The town was Royalton, an exclusive suburb of Chicago.

The hour was the hour of dusk. The occupants of the library were three men, of strikingly different types and appearance.

The first man, tall and thirty-five dressed in gray tweeds, strode up and down in front of the fireplace like an animal in a cage. His face was worn with worry until it looked years older than his body. The second man, big rather than tall, sat stiff and erect in a leather arm chair, his civilian serge outlining his powerful frame with all the authority of a military uniform.

The third man, thin and dark in rusty clericals, who occupied a seat of less dignity, was an individual known to Chicago's church-wise press and public as the Reverend Reuben Acton, meek director of an obscure mission in the slums. More simply and saltily acknowledged as "The

Parson" by his close associates. His face was wide with
shocked amazement.

"What!" he gasped. "Dear Mrs. Edgehill missing—
mysteriously disappeared? I can scarcely believe it! Yet,
'The Lord giveth and the Lord taketh away,'" he recited
with mournful unction. "See Job One Twenty-one. Nevertheless, let us still hope that Mrs. Edgehill may return in
safety. Surely, Chief Connor, had she suffered an accident,
news would have come to us!"

"Maybe so, Mr. Acton. And maybe, 'The Lord taketh
away,' as you put it," offered Royalton's big police chief
dryly. "But it's usually the devil an' not the Lord who asks a
price for the return of stolen property—or persons, rather."

"Yes, kidnaped!" groaned Edgehill. "God help me,
kidnaped! My wife!"

The door of the study flew open

The Parson stared as if thunderstruck. "And—you've already received a demand for ransom?"

"Not that far along," rumbled Connor. "But there's little doubt it'll come soon. Didn't Mr. Edgehill tell you nothing when he called you up in town this afternoon?"

"Only that I might be of some small service to his dear wife, who has always been most generously interested in my modest little mission in the city," blinked The Parson. "So naturally I hastened out to Royalton in the first train I could get."

"I can imagine," said Connor with poorly masked distaste. He glanced at the black bag and broad-brimmed hat parked on the floor. The hat, its concave brim reaching up to the ceiling, looked ludicrously like an appeal to alms.

"Yes, that's all I told him," said Edgehill. "I was afraid to say more than that over the phone, after last night."

"Captain Vindex!"
The Parson said.

"Better tell him now, then. We can't lose no more time."

"As I was explaining before you came, Mr. Acton," responded Edgehill heavily, "my wife left Monday morning for a short visit to her parents in Hennepin, driving herself. It's not a hundred and thirty miles and she should have made it in five hours. I supposed she'd call me up when she got there. She didn't—I mean I got no call. Then I expected a note. When none came by last evening—which would have allowed for every delay even if she had put off writing till Tuesday night—I put in a call for Hennepin. After the children had gone to bed—after nine, I think. You say, Connor, there's only one operator on duty at that hour?"

"After nine, yes, Mr. Edgehill. The night operator, Norah Weldon. We'll check up with her."

"Well, they finally rang me back and I picked up the phone. But it wasn't Hennepin, it was a strange voice. Muffled, yet it sounded nearer, somehow. It said—he said—"

Edgehill stopped, swallowed and stiffened himself.

"He said, 'Keep off the phone, keep off the cops, keep your trap shut—*or else!* You'll get word what to do and when and how to do it, and how much! So watch your step! And don't forget we're watching too!'

"That was all. It sounded—my God, there was no mistaking it, it was nothing but a hellish threat! I knew instantly what it meant. It meant Anne! My wife!"

The Parson drew a sympathetic breath, "And yet, despite that terrifying warning, you ventured to call in the police?"

"I did not!" snapped Edgehill. "I'm strictly obeying orders! But after a night and day of hell, hanging over the phone waiting for a message from the kidnapers that didn't come, I sent word to Connor privately to drop in and see me. Nothing out of the ordinary in that. As a member of the Board of Commissioners here I frequently consult him on one thing or another. I did use the phone to get you. But in your case I figured that even if we're overheard it might do no harm—that it might even be of some advantage."

THE PARSON STILL looked stupid, but receptive.

"In case the snatchers would be listening in, of course," said Connor as sharply as the painful situation permitted. "He means you might be slated to do the Jafsie act over again like you did back on the Bronson an' Harwell cases. Wasn't that the idea, Mr. Edgehill?"

"It was a thin hope," said Edgehill bleakly. "It did occur to me that if anyone were listening in, the kidnapers might remember that as a result of Mr. Acton's intermediation the ransom was promptly paid in those cases, and that both the Bronson and the Harwell child were returned unharmed."

"Yeah, an' that the snatchers got away clean, too, so not even a smell of their identity come through—unless it was to Mr. Acton here!"

The Parson flushed. "And even so, Chief Connor, I should have kept my plighted word not to betray them! Permit me to believe it was my reputation for square dealing among the unhappy sinners I strive with at my mission which induced those whom you mention to, 'Draw near with a true heart in full assurance of faith.' See Hebrews Ten, Verse Twenty. Thus helping to accomplish the rescue of the innocent, the object of all our prayers. Yet fervently as I could wish to be of like service to our beloved Mrs. Edgehill, you must know that unless the Lord should call me, it would be a matter quite beyond my own control."

"Wrong," Connor growled. "It's the devil picks his go-between, not the Lord! Meantime, Mr. Edgehill," he added "if this wire's tapped we ought to know it. Why not call up the phone company an' get a repairman?"

"No," said Edgehill flatly. "If those fiends can communicate as they did last night, in God's name let them! I want no obstruction put in their way. Not in *any* way!"

Connor shook his head. "You can't expect results if we sit on the sidelines while them devils get away with murder! If only you had told me last night the minute you got that call—"

"To *help* them get away with murder? Tell you about it while that hellish warning was still ringing on the wire? Good God, do you think I'm crazy? Understand, Connor, there's to be no police interference in this case at all! I want my wife back."

"Well then, if you're afraid of the police buttin' in, Mr. Edgehill, why not call Washin'ton. The D. of J. would have the Chicago branch on the wire in ten minutes, an' there'd be a flock of Federal ops out here quicker than you'd think. And believe me," Connor urged earnestly, "they're real bloodhounds, those boys. The snatch gangs hate the Federal heat worse than hellfire. It's ten to one, accordin' to the records, they'd nail whoever snatched Mrs. Edgehill, even if it took a year. They get their man!"

"Yes, but how about Mrs. Edgehill?" anxiously interposed The Parson. "Would they be sure to get dear Mrs. Edgehill also?"

Connor hesitated—hardened. "Chances are, yes."

"And I'll take *no* chances!" glared Edgehill. "Chances are they'd kill her as soon as they found I'd disobeyed orders and they were being hunted! Forget you're a cop, Connor, and be human! Tell me what you'd do yourself in my place."

"That's a tough one, Mr. Edgehill." Connor reddened. "I am a cop. Seven years I pounded the bricks; eight was I a Chicago dick, both plain an' fancy; an' for another six I run the bureau—till you brought me out here to run Royalton. So I've had plenty experience of all kinds, includin' the snatch racket."

"You haven't answered by question!"

"I'M ANSWERIN' IT. All right, then, if Mrs. Edgehill was my Ellen an' I was you—or had the money you got—I'd tell police an' Feds both to go clean to hell. I'd shut my mouth good an' tight like I'd been told, so help me, an' pay quick when the time come. I ought to resign for admittin' it, but it's only sound sense, more shame to it! Because them devils can always kill when they can't collect—or is chased. The deck is stacked from the bottom up against the rest of us."

"My judgment also, Chief Connor," said The Parson softly. "It is surely the safest course under the circumstances. Even the Good Book advises it. See Isaiah Thirty-five, Verse Ten, 'And the ransomed shall return, and sorrow and sighing shall flee away.' A prophecy I myself have seen verified more than once."

"An' so you have," said Connor grimly.

Edgehill was silent for a moment. "So that's the answer," he said at last. "You have no help to offer, either of you."

"I'll drop in on Norah Weldon this evening," Connor volunteered. "She should know what broke in on you last night, an' how to fix it so's she could locate any call like it without anybody's gettin' wise. That might help some."

"Yet women are but frail vessels," meekly suggested The Parson. "You'd have to explain, and mightn't she then be tempted to gossip about this sad but sensational event?"

"I can scare the life out of her," Connor frowned. "I might even sick the priest on her. She wouldn't talk then."

The Parson's eyes narrowed. "That's an idea," he agreed. "A priest! Women are commonly susceptible to the dictates of their religion, but particularly so, I have found, to those of its consecrated representatives. If Miss Weldon is visited by a servant of the Lord, I'll warrant she will prove as discreet as myself."

Something sensed rather than heard in The Parson's voice caused Connor to look up sharply. "Hmph!" he grunted. "I hope it will be the other way round, too— intendin' no offense."

"None taken," smiled The Parson gently. "I hope I am proof against all honest but mistaken suspicion."

Edgehill raised his head— "And you be careful, Connor! Don't forget what it means to me! I'd die ten times over rather than have anything happen to my wife—anything *more!*" He winced. "God, how long must I wait to learn what has happened already?"

2

THE NOTE OF DOOM

HE HAD HARDLY finished speaking before there came a light tap at the door. He answered it, to return with a yellow envelope and an ashen face.

"A telegram!" he said hoarsely, staring at it as if he had never seen such a thing before. It trembled in his hand. Suddenly he tore it open, and the look of apprehension on his face became complicated with mystification.

"Rubies!" he ejaculated. "A hundred and fifty thousand and—rubies!"

"What's that?" asked Connor.

"Listen," choked Edgehill.

> PRICE FOR ABOVE RUBIES HUNDRED FIFTY
> THOUSAND—POINT—HOLDING IN ESCROW
> FOR QUICK SETTLEMENT—POINT—DETAILS
> BY MAIL.

"Rubies!" repeated the astonished Connor. "At a hundred an' fifty grand—what's it mean? That's a power of rubies. You sure it's for you, Mr. Edgehill? Who's it from?"

"I don't understand—or I hope to God I don't! But it's

addressed to me, and it was filed at South Bend an hour ago. But there's no signature."

Connor blinked. "It's a fake, maybe. There's no jewelry store in South Bend that's that strong!"

"May I see it?" asked The Parson soberly. "Thank you… Ah," he coughed, "I think I have it. It would seem to be the very news you were waiting for, dear Mr. Edgehill. The keyword—rubies—might prove puzzling to one not intimate with Holy Writ, but I judge it to be a reference to the blessed words of King Lemuel in Proverbs Thirty-one, the Tenth Verse, 'Who can find a virtuous woman? for her price is far above rubies.' The word *for* in the telegram being an obvious misspelling for *far*. The rest, I am afraid, clearly means that she is being held captive—or in escrow, as they put it—until payment of the sum mentioned."

Connor stared at The Parson with a little more respect.

"You've hit it, Mr. Acton," he admitted.

"Only because I am more or less familiar with the Word of God," deprecated The Parson. "It attaches to my profession."

"But hell!" gritted Connor. "Even usin' the Bible to help put over their dirty wickedness, the blasphemin' devils! An' the message safe as a church, at that, seein' nobody would suspect it to be the voice of a snatch racket soundin' off. Well, anyway, Mr. Edgehill, it's a start."

Edgehill slowly focused despairing eyes on him. "Not a start," he said thickly. "It's the finish. I couldn't raise, beg, borrow or steal a fifth of that sum!"

Even The Parson's jaw dropped. Connor stared, dumfounded.

Edgehill's forehead glistened with cold sweat. "You think

me rich?" he said hoarsely. "Still rich? But you must know how the bottom's dropped out of everything. Investments, business, property—*everything!* Even my real estate's not worth the mortgages written on it, so the banks won't relieve me of it!

"For two years I've been borrowing steadily and heavily, trying to keep on going in the hope things would get better. The only protection left for my family today is my insurance—if I can manage to keep it paid up. Protection!" he repeated violently. "What a hideous mockery! It's my wife's life that's threatened, when if I'd been kidnaped or killed myself she could have looked forward to the very amount they're demanding for her."

"O' course I knew you'd been cuttin' down on servants an' expenses generally, Mr. Edgehill," breathed Connor. "Everybody's doin' that, even here in Royalton. But I never suspicioned it was that bad with you!"

"What a very distressing situation!" said The Parson with tremulous solicitude. "And yet how boldly, how shrewdly have you concealed your difficulties from the world, dear Mr. Edgehill! I mean—your continued prominence in affairs, your way of living, even this costly and beautiful estate—"

"I've been bluffing it out, of course, up to now," Edgehill groaned. "You know—show your wounds and the pack tears you to pieces. But see what it has brought me to!"

"Yea, verily," sighed The Parson piously, though his eyes glittered. " 'The pride of thine heart hath deceived thee.' See Obadiah, Verse Three. Yet the chief misfortune is that by your heroic and excusable deceit the wicked also have been led astray. There is the problem that confronts us!"

"Don't I realize it? Connor," entreated Anne Edgehill's miserable husband, "is there a chance that those fiends might be persuaded to free my wife for the utmost sum I could raise—say possibly thirty thousand dollars?"

Connor fiddled with his watch chain. "Better let me start things goin' here, Mr. Edgehill," he said quietly. "An' call up Washin'ton."

EDGEHILL SLUMPED IN his seat. "I understand," he said in a ghastly voice. "Go ahead, then. Possibly they'll kill her quicker and more mercifully than they would if I stalled and haggled with them to no result."

Connor would have babbled some weak reassurance. But it died in his throat. "We'll do the best we can," he said huskily. "I—Mrs. Edgehill was a sweet lady! By *God!*" he exploded. "We're practically helpless, the way we stand! If only some miracle of wholesale skunk-killin' could happen here like it happened in New York in that Perham case a few weeks ago. That's the sort o' thing ought to happen!"

The Parson rose half way from his chair as if on slow springs. Then he sank as slowly back again, unnoticed.

"I read about it," said Edgehill dully. "Two gangs of kidnapers got to slaughtering each other, and the victim—a child—was lucky enough to be saved from between them. Was that it?"

"Yes. Like a bone from between two fightin' dogs," nodded Connor. "Only"—his forehead wrinkled—"it wasn't that way, either. It couldn't have been! Because this mob that had stole the kid—seven of 'em, includin' a woman and the president of a big bank who was proved to have been peddler to the mob—was found laid out in a row deader than a herring, each an' every one of 'em with a big red V burned into their forehead, while the kid come home with the milkman, alive an' well.

"Nobody knew who had brought her! Figure that out! Yes, an' come to think," Connor turned to look at The Parson, "three o' them dead birds was identified as punks an' muscle men from Chicago. Maybe some of your choice parishioners down to the mission, Mr. Acton!"

The Parson

"I don't think so. I saw the names. I didn't recognize any of them," said The Parson, shaking his head.

"Well," said Connor, "that V... I got a hunch it might have been the sign of some new crowd that was takin' things into their own hands. That it might have stood for somethin' like 'vigilante.'"

"Vindex!" burst out The Parson, utterly unable to withhold the accursed word.

"Huh?" Connor whirled in swift surprise. "What's that mean?"

"Vengeance—the Avenger." The Reverend Reuben Acton forced a smile.

"It's a good-soundin' word," admitted Connor. "You got the advantage of me on that Bible stuff. If it means what you say it does, it suits me. But we only got ourselves to depend on," he said regretfully, with a glance at Edgehill. "I better get about it."

"May I say just this?" pleaded The Parson, partially recovered from his shock. "According to the telegram, dear Mr. Edgehill, you should receive a letter of instructions in a day or so. And the letter might even mention a chosen intermediary. Might it not be wise to wait at least until the letter comes before enlisting the law? For in the meantime I shall pray most fervently, and it might be that I should become inspired—I mean that the Lord would show His mercy unto us."

Edgehill grasped at the straw. "Yes, hold up until we hear further, Connor," he said feverishly. "If they should happen to select Mr. Acton—they might know about him—trust him—even believe what he could tell them about the money. To call in the police is almost sure murder!"

"Well, it's for you to decide, Mr. Edgehill, an' not for me to stand out against you," said Connor. "I suppose we're between the devil an' the deep sea, anyhow. I can still be puttin' my head or my hand to somethin'. Like Norah Weldon, for instance… You goin' back to town, Mr. Acton? My car's here. I'll drive you to the station. That your bag?"

"Some slight paraphernalia of my calling," said The Parson meekly. "Ministers to the soul, like those to the body, should go prepared for every emergency."

3

THE KING OF HEARTS

AT THE RAILROAD station Connor let The Parson out.
Frowning, the latter watched the policeman drive away.
Then he entered the station and bought his ticket to
Chicago, learning that it would be some forty minutes
before there was a train.

That was time enough to tuck in a visit, if he could
manage it unobserved. For Connor's proposal to question
the night operator on the subject of the interrupted call to
Hennepin had disturbed him. And, thought The Parson
grimly, if a priest were the surest means of keeping the girl
silent, he himself could hand her some priestly admonition
that would prevent her from talking, even to a cop!

He observed that Royalton's railroad station boasted no
package locker. So he crossed the waiting room to a door
marked GENTS and passed through it, finding himself
alone. On the entrance to one of the interior compartments
hung a card bearing the legend: *Out of order.*

The Parson grinned at this unexpected bit of luck and
eased into the next compartment. Three minutes later he
emerged in a plain business suit that was not black, while
the brim of a gray felt shadowed his face which was sufficiently altered. His clerical costume, hat and all, reposed

under cover of the bag in a far corner of the compartment. Wedging the door behind him with a waste newspaper, he transferred the *Out of order* sign from one door to the other.

In another five minutes he entered the hallway of a cheap flat in Royalton's business section. After glancing at the names and numbers on the letter boxes he climbed two flights up and tapped on a door inscribed 3-B.

When it opened it was but half way, and as if reluctantly. In the opening, holding to the door, stood a girl with Irish blue eyes and with hair and complexion both over-bright. Yet she made a not unpleasant picture in the gay knit stuff that caressed every line of her slender body.

"Miss Weldon?" beamed The Parson, removing his hat with a flourish.

"Still," said the girl flippantly. "But engaged. Who shall I say good-by to?"

"Let's see," said The Parson, still beaming. "Well, you might say it to Mrs. Edgehill... May I come in?"

Norah Weldon gasped as if he had punched her in the stomach. The blood fled from her cheeks, leaving paint alone on garish exhibition. Even her impudent little figure, like her impudent assurance, became deflated.

"Who are—you?" she asked faintly. Then her panic raised its voice. "Willie!" she called.

The Parson, preparing to edge past her, paused. Another figure appeared behind the girl, to glower over her shoulder at the intruder.

"What's it?" snapped the newcomer. "Oh—*jeeze!*"

"Well, well, *well!*" exclaimed The Parson. "If it isn't Sweet William, King of Hearts! What a surprise!"

The startled punk backed up and squeezed out a smile.

"Why, hello, boss! 'S all right, kid, it's the big-shot. Come right in, boss! I—we was just going to have a little eats before Norah here has to get back on the job. Sit in with us!"

"Thank you, William," said The Parson, closing the door behind him. "I'm catching a train, but I'd like to hold brief converse with both of you. Bless me how cozy and domestic," he added as he looked over the tiny living room, its center table set with dishes and a bottle of wine. "No wonder you forgot the chief essential of your only useful talent as King of Hearts, William. To say a clean good-by even to the juciest blossom after sucking all the juice out of it!"

Norah Weldon, still under the shock of The Parson's suggestion at her outer door, gave a start.

The dapper gangster colored. "Aw, I just drove out this after' to—to keep an eye on the job, boss. Just to make sure things was goin' all right."

"Thoughtful of you," said The Parson ironically. "Especially as it involved the sacrifice of that quick trip out of town I had recommended. Let's hope your disinterested action doesn't cost you anything. Because things are going very badly."

"They—they are?" stammered Willie, losing his color.

"And so I came to inform Miss Weldon. The main bull of this town is going to put the screws on her about some phony phone calls last night, and he plans to catch her when she goes on duty."

THE GIRL BLEATED. The gangster blinked incredulously. "You mean that sap Edgehill has beefed to the law after my scarin' him off over the phone, Parson? Why, I give him word for word what you give me to give him, through a han'kerchief an' all, right here in this room the minute she hooked me on from the office while he was waitin' for long distance! Why—*hell!*"

He turned on Norah in panic fury. "Answer that, you dirty slut!" he spat at her. "Wasn't it *you* tol' me them two was just two damn fools for love—so mushy they was a hot joke all over town? Wasn't it *you* picked on 'em for a natural that couldn't go wrong, because he was just as loose with kale as he was rotten with it? An' here first thing he does is set the bulls on us!"

"But he wouldn't! Mr. Edgehill couldn't!" wailed Norah, terrified. "I tell you they *are* like that, honest-to-God sweeties all the time! Just like you and me, Willie darling!" she put in with frantic adjuration. "I told you the truth! He's got money to burn and he'd never let any harm come to her—or I'd never have done it, not even for you, Willie! *Willie!* Oh, my God, don't look at me that way! Haven't I done everything you said, Willie? Haven't I?"

"Handsome, but heartless as well as brainless, you see," The Parson observed to the sobbing girl. "That's what makes him King of Hearts. And *you*, punk, listen to *me!*" he barked. "I planted you here to do your Romeo act and work some soft skirt for a ripe lead, and you pick a fool that puts the finger on a false front—on a fake who's hardly able to raise the ransom for a yellow dog! So—*what?*"

Willie's fury curdled into fear. But The Parson's assertion was too preposterous to swallow without expostulation.

"Jeeze, boss," he stammered, "why—why, he rates a gold mine, that guy Edgehill does! Honest! Why anybody'll tell you—"

"I'm telling you!" said The Parson dangerously. "I know!"

"Sure you know, boss," Willie hastily agreed. "I wouldn't dispute you, only—only how would I know? Didn't I have to take the kid's word for it? She'd ought to of known. She's living here long enough!"

"You said it—she's lived here long *enough!* As King Solomon said before you," The Parson droned ominously. " 'A false witness shall perish.' See Proverbs Twenty-one, Verse Twenty-eight."

Willie shivered.

Norah cowered trembling in a corner, her tongue stricken with the impotence peculiar to a nightmare. And nightmare it was, into which her shabby dream of love had so suddenly been transformed. She wanted to scream, but the only sound she could produce was a strangled moan.

The Parson grinned. "And I see that, as usual, you're dressed to kill, William," he said with crystal-clear significance. "Even to a sweet-scented silk handkerchief smelling up your breast pocket. So go ahead and use it."

Willie's forehead broke out into a fine perspiration.

"Aw, boss," he mumbled shakily, "she's a good kid. Couldn't we—"

The Parson stretched his grin only a very little further, but it turned his face into the savage semblance of a dog's. His eyes glowed, while the skin wrinkled away from his teeth and gums. One look was enough for the King of Hearts. Willie gasped, turned and started to cross the room, drawing the bright silk handkerchief as he went.

Norah Weldon came out of her nightmare. Although her lover's intention showed plainly enough in his frozen face and his ferret eyes, she leaped and flung her arms about him, at the same time loosing a loud shriek of terror. The punk quenched it almost before it began by thrusting the heel of a hand against her chin and clamping down on her nose and mouth. But she still managed a broken babble against his palm.

"Willie! Oh, God—don't—darling—"

He whirled her about and whipped the handkerchief around her neck with a single motion, seizing its ends with opposite hands and pulling it taut. More taut. One dreadful minute passed.

"Hurry!" urged The Parson. "Time's short!"

Norah hung from the handkerchief, her knees sagging. Her face grew purple and her eyes and tongue protruded horribly. Her lungs wheezed a little, and her fluttering fingers drummed a tiny tattoo on the empty air. Then the wheezing and the drumming stopped.

"I guess that's all," nodded The Parson.

THE KING OF HEARTS promptly let go an end of the handkerchief; The girl's body slumped to the floor. Willie mopped his wet forehead with the fragrant instrument of death and stuffed it back into his pocket with trembling fingers. "J-jeeze," he chattered. "That was—tough!"

"*You're* still alive," The Parson reminded him dryly. "And now you won't have to face the cops. The only witness against you is taken care of. Connor would have turned her inside out."

"Hell!" stared Willie. "That's right, too. I hadn't thought o' that!"

"You dumb punks that think you're hard-boiled make me sick," said The Parson disgustedly. "It's only your brains that are hard-boiled—like an egg! Listen, have you a car here?"

"Sure! It's round a corner three blocks off. I've took good care not to show myself with the kid, boss. Not to make no talk, you know. So that's all right," Willie hastened to reassure him. "You want to ride back with me?"

"No! I told you I was going in by train. But I want to see you in town when I get there. No more need of your hiding out in the country now," said The Parson with an unmoved glance at what lay on the floor. "And you can easily beat the train in."

"Oh, sure!"

"I may have to get hold of some of the outside mob," explained The Parson. "As I told you, things have changed."

Willie's face faded a little. "Yeah… say, boss, I forgot… I was goin' to tell you," he stammered, fearful lest he had imperiled his restoration to good standing, "that I met a guy this morning who wants to see you an' you might want to see him. I seen him in Sam's Place on South Halstead. You know him. He's a smart gun. He might fit, for one."

"Who was it, you fool?"

"Oh, sure! It was Gordon—Foxie Gordon," answered Willie nervously. "Him who was in New York with you an' Canty on that—say, what's the matter, boss? What's wrong?"

The Parson was staring at him as if he were a ghost. "You—saw—Foxie Gordon?" he demanded harshly. "Foxie Gordon got his head blown off in New York!"

The King of Hearts burst into an amazing cackle. It relieved him immensely to discover that whatever break had upset The Parson wasn't of his making. "I know he did.

I told him so! 'So what the hell you doin' here, Foxie,' I ast him. But Foxie ast me back again. 'How the hell would they, identify a guy that took a clip o' slugs in the back o' the nut?' says Foxie. 'He wouldn't have no face left to know him by, would he?'

"An' that's right, boss, I've seen 'em that way. Why, you wouldn't know your own mother without any face! Foxie says they got him wrong. It must of been some other guy, that's all. I guess Foxie knows if he's dead or if he's alive, don't he? Anyways, *I* know him!" And Willie cackled again, freely.

The Reverend Reuben Acton uttered a sizzling string of imprecations that couldn't have been quoted from Job in the latter's direst vexation and adversity.

Certain of Foxie Gordon's death, The Parson instantly and venomously mentalized the unknown avenger who, in New York a month earlier, had first killed and then impersonated Cantwell, The Parson's own right bower, and who next had added insult to injury by an impossible escape from a consummate trap!

Who had frustrated a perfectly contrived abduction, rescued its victim and robbed The Parson himself of an already collected ransom of a hundred thousand dollars. Who had sealed the outrage with a clean sweep of seven more killings, burning his ghastly symbol—V—into the foreheads of the dead!

That mysterious executioner from whom he himself had barely escaped alive at the last—the mere mention of whose terrible activities by Chief Connor had wrenched from The Parson's momentarily loosened tongue the accursed name of VINDEX.

The Parson's eyes burned Willie through and through. Then he spoke:

"You're right. I want to see him! Find him and send him to me!" Then, remembering his train, The Parson, turned and hurried from the flat.

"Jeeze, can you beat that?" said Willie, softly, staring after him in blank amazement and with keen uneasiness. "Looks like Foxie's got somethin' comin' to him! Hell, is it my fault he didn't get croaked?"

Norah Weldon made no answer. But the faintest of shadows on the down-drawn shade at the window vanished as if it had been her lingering spirit.

4

THE FIVE AVENGERS

ARNOLD BRENT, ONCE famous on the stage for his
remarkable character parts and his facile and perfect imitations, his role now forever limited to the tragic character
and alias of Captain Vindex, entered a tenth floor, suite in
the Blackstone Hotel an hour before midnight.

His three fellow victims of kidnapers and sworn associates awaited him—big Steve Burns, ex-secret service agent;
Dr. Robert Ellsworth, some few years before noted as a
surgeon; and Edwin Thrale, a former lawyer of equal reputation. Each of them, like their leader, self-dedicated to a
lifetime of ruthless vengeance and extermination against
the snatch racket, which had robbed them of all they had
once loved and lived for.

Kato, yellow shadow to Captain Vindex, ex-dresser, valet
and unforgetting idolator of two vanished little children,
hovered in the background.

"Well?" asked Captain Vindex.

Burns shook his head. "Just about like you said it would
be, when we come on here to hunt that devil down in his
hole. Even the police don't seem to have any suspicion that
he's anything but the Reverend Reuben Acton, who runs
his little mission down on the South Side. All they got

against him is that he deals with a lot of tough babies they'd love to lay their saps on, an' that he's acted a couple o' times as go-between in some big snatch, like Jafsie in the Lindbergh case. Made the deal an' handled the money. But he come through with it an' got back the victims they couldn't find themselves, so they got nothing on him for that."

"Which seems to be the case with other citizens who know anything about him," said Thrale in his precise voice. "Even with some of the local ministers. While none of them would visit the mission or touch The Parson's protégés with a ten-foot pole, they actually seem to admire him for his gutter-sweeping Christianity. And they credit his success in those go-between cases to his mission connections and to his wholesome influence among the criminal element."

"Could he have a more perfect setup?" shrugged Captain Vindex. "Thanks to the mission his position is almost impregnable. He can run with the hare and chase with the hounds unsuspected. It takes supreme nerve and intelligence, but we know he has both."

"And we know also *who* and *what* he is!" flared Dr. Ellsworth, his eyes burning and his long fingers writhing and contracting ominously. "And so does the underworld, or a good part of it! Knows that under cover of his hellish hypocrisy he's a real king of the snatch racket—that he deals in blood and tears! Why can't we openly denounce him? Or cut him down the minute we can locate and identify him? Wasn't that why we came on here from New York, since he slipped out of our hands in the Perham case?"

"For several reasons," said Captain Vindex dryly. "First, because he undoubtedly knows we're here and is holed up. Or is disguised and guarded, with unknown fingers on a dozen triggers. Second, because ever since we struck the first blow at the snatch racket and at The Parson—to avenge our intolerable wrongs and to do what we could to prevent others from suffering what we have suffered—we've been outside the law ourselves. We're outlaws just as much as are any kidnapers. Legally, we too are killers, with seven lives to our credit already. Hardly a situation in which our denunciation, unsupported by absolute proof, would hold water. Or one in which we could shoot down in the streets of Chicago a man accepted as one of its most Christian citizens."

"Credit is right!" barked Burns. "What have we been killin' but wolves an' rattlesnakes? The scum o' the earth? Kidnapers? Good God, if the police an' even the government can't do a decent job at it, somebody's got to? They'd ought to give us a gold medal for every one of 'em!"

"Thirdly and finally," went on Captain Vindex, ignoring the outbreak, "because our first obligation is to rescue the innocent without endangering them before punishing the guilty. The Parson has just engineered another big kidnaping."

There was a gasp of astonishment. Burns stared with his mouth open.

"Well, that seems to be his business," he said at last. "But how come you know about it after bein' in this town less'n twenty-four hours, like the rest of us, Captain Vindex?"

"Capta'n crazy like hell!" Kato shrilled. "He put on Foxie Gordon one more time an' tell me stay here! How I follow? I not know Tchicago!"

"You *what?* While we was snoopin' round after general information like a bunch of rookies you—"

"I thought I'd see if I couldn't run into some of The Parson's old muscle men who might talk to Foxie Gordon," shrugged Captain Vindex. "And I was lucky. I did."

"CRAZY IS RIGHT! An' lucky, too!" Burns shook his head. "Why, all the papers had it in New York when Foxie Gordon was killed, an' The Parson himself was in town. An' do you think they wouldn't know it here?"

"A mad risk to take!" objected Ellsworth, perturbed.

"Just a minute, Doctor," said Vindex. "How was Gordon killed?"

"Why Cantwell told us he'd emptied a gun into the back of Gordon's head when he found he'd been secretly dickering with you."

"Yes. And what would that do to a man's face?"

"There wouldn't be any left," admitted Ellsworth. "But—"

"Just the argument I used on Sweet William at a bar on South Halstead Street," smiled Captain Vindex grimly. "And I made it stick. Then after a few drinks to celebrate my revival, he spilled something to an old pal. Without exactly intending to."

"Sweet William?" snapped Burns. "Him they used to call King of Hearts? I knew that load of hydrophobia back when I was in the service. He could make any woman think he was Clark Gable an' Morgan Rockefeller rolled into one, an' then turn her inside out from brains to pocketbook; That the guy?"

"The same. And now working for The Parson."

"The hell he is!"

"Yes. Willie's none too bright inside, though outwardly he resembles Solomon in all his glory. He hinted broadly about some new snatch, knowing I'd been a finger for The Parson—Gordon had been, that is—and then gave me the slip. Or tried to. But I trailed him out to a place called Royalton, where I found out more about it, and ended by walking in on a killing connected with the snatch itself."

The three were speechless.

"I even put the mark on her forehead," said Captain Vindex gravely. "When the Parson hears of it he'll know we're here. He may know now."

"Her forehead?" stared Thrale. "A woman?"

"A telephone operator whom Sweet William had evidently persuaded to peddle one of the town's rich men. The name is Edgehill. It's his wife that's just been kidnaped. But The Parson didn't trust the girl, and ordered Willie to kill her. Willie did."

"The Parson?" Burns started violently. "You mean—"

"He was there, too," said Captain Vindex dryly. "I didn't see him, but I heard him. And Willie addressed him that way once or twice. And I'd know that devil's voice among a thousand. The first time I heard it, if you remember, I thought it was the last thing I was ever going to hear on earth."

Thrale frowned. "Tell us how it happened, won't you?"

"Oh, Willie went to this girl's flat in a cheap part of Royalton. So did I, only he went up the stairs and I found a fire escape that ran just outside a back window. The Parson showed up a little later, to their surprise as much as to mine, apparently. To tell them about some suspicious telephone calls to Edgehill, and that the police were due to question her. That's why they killed her. Afraid she'd break and spill."

"And you didn't see him?" asked Burns.

"The shade was down. But I opened the window an inch to hear."

"And then what?"

"Willie and The Parson went, The Parson first. Then I slipped into the room to see just what had happened. The girl had been strangled."

There was a short silence. Then Burns cleared his throat. "So what do we do?" he asked in a troubled voice. "I don't have to tell you, Captain Vindex, that The Parson's a fast worker and a good guesser. Willie likely told him he'd met you, or Foxie Gordon, rather."

"He did. I heard him."

"Yeah. I was afraid of it... Well, The Parson don't know how you look in your own face, that's one comfort. But he'll know well enough, from the Cantwell impersonation in New York, who 'Foxie' was."

"Exactly. And that's the only sure way of getting in touch with him and with the Edgehill kidnaping gang."

"I don't like it. It's too dangerous," said Burns uncomfortably. "The word'll be all over town to get 'Foxie' on sight."

"Mind telling me what you're driving at?" asked Ellsworth.

"Oh, nothin' at all," frowned Burns. "Nothin' at all—excep' we're supposed to set a trap for them damned rats an' bait it with Captain Vindex in the shape o' Foxie Gordon—his third and last appearance in the part, or I miss my guess. That's all!"

"It sounds like suicide," said Thrale.

"Don't I know it?" Burns agreed.

"On the contrary, it's our only chance," said Captain

Vindex evenly. "Not only of getting in first blow, but also of discovering and saving the kidnaped woman. It's a question of finding Willie once more, for The Parson didn't tell him anything about the impersonation. And if, as you said, The Parson's a fast worker, we'll have to work faster, that's all."

"Have to be fast enough to beat a bullet," muttered Burns. "Okay, then Captain Vindex. But this time 'Foxie' gets a bodyguard! When is it?"

"Tonight," said Vindex.

AN HOUR LATER Foxie Gordon, seemingly a little unsure of himself at both extremities but very sure of himself in all other particulars, reentered Sam's Place on South Halstead Street after a last quick glance at a big sedan parked in a dark spot across the street. He knew that car; he had followed it in a taxi for twenty miles a dozen hours earlier.

At the bar he wedged himself in between a pair of sharp-eyed punks who made prompt room for him. He responded to their somewhat startled greetings by a generous gesture taking in the whole long line-up.

"Set 'em up all-roun', Nosie! Ever'body in. 'S on me!"

Foxie's two flankers exchanged sardonic grins across the back of his neck. A dozen other men in the place watched him with an assortment of mocking sneers. But they all drank with haste and willingness.

"Shet 'em up again!" crowed Foxie, sliding a twenty after his empty glass.

"Big-hearted as hell for a stiff, ain't he?" grinned the man at his right. "Looks like they planted him without friskin' him—hey, Foxie?"

"Aw, leave him blow it before he goes back," winked Foxie's left-hand neighbor. "Seein's he can't blow it there, he can't blow it fast enough. Pretty dry where you come from, eh, Foxie?" he cackled.

"A-ah, cut it!" drooled Foxie. "That stuff'sh shtale! Gawd, can't a guy ever prove he ain't been croaked? I been tryin' all roun' thish town ever shinsh—"

He broke off suddenly to peer drunkenly up and down the bar. "Willie c'n tell you—where'sh Willie? I wash tellin' him all 'bout it—today. Ri' here! Where'sh Willie?"

A message passed over some grapevine telegraph line to Sam's back room, and its door opened. On the threshold stood Sweet William, King of Hearts. As he caught sight of Foxie Gordon a cynical smile passed over his face. Then, wriggling his wasp-waisted coat into a more perfect set, twitching the perfumed silk handkerchief in his breast pocket half an inch higher and cocking his cream-colored felt at a slightly snappier angle, he moved down along the bar.

"Hyah, Foxie!"

"Hey, here he ish!" cackled Foxie, teetering backward. "Lookin' f'you all over lot shinsh aft'noon—or wash it morning? Nev' min'... Here we are! Have li'l' drink, Willie?"

"Not now, kid," grinned Willie. "Nor you better not have no more, not now. Wanter come along with me? Somebody wants to see you, guy."

"I know," said Foxie, trying to hold himself straight. "Parshon wantsh shee *me*—an' I wantsh shee *him!*"

The whole bar went silent. The pair on each side of Foxie edged toward him, but Willie waved them back.

"I don't need no help with this souse, 'less I have to carry him across the street!" he muttered. "Come on, souse, I got a car over there. We ride."

Clinging to Willie's arm, Foxie staggered out through the door, across the sidewalk and across the street. But within three feet of the big sedan he became instantaneously and miraculously sober.

"KEEP YOUR MOUTH shut! Not a yip!" he ordered in a voice that froze Sweet William's blood. And at the same moment Willie noticed a small figure rise behind the wheel of his own car, while the rear door opened to show three shadowy faces inside.

"In you go!"

Willie pitched in, aided from both front and rear. "Foxie Gordon" leaped into the front seat beside the driver, and the car started. In the darkness behind, a hand not his own was emptying Willie's shoulder holster, and two hard elbows were pressing him back into the seat.

Somebody pulled down the window shades and switched on the dome light. From across the back of the front seat the transformed "Foxie Gordon" was regarding Willie with eyes that simply terrified him.

"We're taking you on a little ride, way out of town where it's quiet, punk. And where you're going to tell us all about the Edgehill snatch. Everything!"

All the red that still distinguished the King of Hearts turned to a sickly gray. "What—whatcher mean?" he croaked.

"You told me first!" said Captain Vindex icily. "And you're going to tell me more! I was there when you talked with The Parson and strangled the girl late this afternoon, too, if it interests you!"

"You—there?" gurgled Willie. "I—who—who are you? The devil himself?"

"Ask The Parson. You'll meet him soon in hell, I hope. But your present concern is to decide just how you want to die. That will depend entirely on how your tongue wags."

"The hell!" said Sweet William a little more stoutly, beginning to get over his first shock of surprise. "If you're dicks you gotter turn me in. You can't croak me! That ain't the law, it's murder! An' I got a mouthpiece an' a big one! The Parson'll get hold of him for me. He'll have me out—"

Captain Vindex smiled. "We'll want to know him. You can tell us all about him, too."

"Henry Mandel, that's who it is," sneered Willie. "Wait'll you get up against that guy! Huh? Doncher know who he is?" The evident absence of effect caused by that momentous name puzzled and disturbed him. "Ain't you guys dicks?" he weakened.

"See? He can't take it," growled Burns from close beside him. "He'll squeal like a rat!"

"The hell I will!" snarled Willie. "I ain't no snitch! Try an' see!"

"Just what we're going to do," said Captain Vindex.

5

THE DEVIL'S WHISPER

AT HALF PAST ten the following evening The Parson walked unobtrusively up the long Edgehill driveway. He was there by appointment. He now felt reasonably assured that despite the disconcerting revelation of Edgehill's inability to pay the ransom demanded for his kidnaped wife, the problem had been solved for him.

Solved for everybody concerned, indeed, and most satisfactorily. The kidnapers would finally obtain that envisioned but suddenly doubtful hundred and fifty thousand, thanks to the advice and co-operation of the boldest and smartest legal mind in Chicago. Dear Mrs. Edgehill would regain her freedom—for what it might be worth to her! And, once Albert Edgehill had been brought to see the point, he would naturally and gratefully, as a devoted husband, choose his wife's security in preference to his own.

The Parson looked sharply about him into the darkness as he ascended the driveway. One small cog in his machinery seemed still to be missing. Sweet William, King of Hearts, who had been assigned to meet him in that darkness, didn't seem to be on hand. The Parson damned both

THE BRAND OF VINDEX

him and his absence heartily, but proceeded, being due himself.

If Willie should turn up a few moments late, he would know how to get in and how to behave himself. Besides, the more he thought of it, the more The Parson trusted his machinery to run smoothly even without that extra cog. He had a full and sufficient faith in the compelling exigencies of the situation.

Edgehill admitted The Parson personally, welcoming him as a drowning man might welcome even a waterlogged crate in the middle of the ocean. He led his visitor into the library and closed the door.

"No one can hear us," he said. "The children are asleep on the other side of the house and the two servants are in their own wing in the rear. I told them to stay there. As you advised, Mr. Acton, complete secrecy may be the safest thing."

"You're not expecting Chief Connor?"

"No." Edgehill winced. "For some reason Connor seems to be returning to his earlier opinion regarding the advisability of bringing in the police. You haven't seen him? Then you haven't heard—"

With trembling fingers he handed The Parson a piece of brown paper pasted over with words clipped from newspapers.

"This was found shoved under a back door this morning. It names you as go-between, you see, so you're my last hope, Mr. Acton! If you can't persuade those devils to release my poor wife for what I can pay I'm afraid it's all over. In God's name, tell me you're going to act for me— that you'll save her!"

The Parson looked at the message.

"You may rest assured I'll do my very utmost, dear Mr. Edgehill," he responded with unction. "For I feel as you do about calling in the police, despite our good Chief Connor's professional bias in their favor. Nevertheless, it becomes my painful duty to tell you"—The Parson raised sympathetic eyes—"that so far it appears impossible to persuade those desperate villains of your incapacity to pay the great sum they demand."

Edgehill stared at him. "Great God!" he croaked. "You mean you've already been in touch with them?"

"By telephone even this very morning. Yes," sighed The Parson. "And I entreated them to grant me an opportunity to explain your unfortunate situation. I offered to meet them in person and alone, committing myself to their perilous mercies in order to try and convince them of the truth! I appealed to their hard hearts, to their inmost conscience, to their hope of salvation in the hereafter! Yet they but mocked me as the children of evil mocked at the Prophet Elisha. See Second Kings Two, Verse Twenty-three. They said to me, like the doubting Didymus, 'I will not believe.'"

For ten seconds the library was silent.

"My God!" whispered Edgehill at last.

"And within twenty-four hours from tonight," continued The Parson in tones of tenderest commiseration, "I must be able to report that arrangements for payment of the full sum demanded are in train, or—"

"Or what?"

The Parson spread out his hands helplessly, with tears in his eyes and in his voice. "Or cruel harm is threatened to the sweet Mrs. Edgehill! May the Lord forgive them for such great wickedness!"

"May God send them to uttermost hell for it!" cried Edgehill harshly, his face contorted with agony.

"Christian though I am, I could almost join with you in that unChristian yet excusable supplication," confessed The Parson, with a quick look of triumphant satisfaction at Edgehill, who had buried his face in his hands.

"TELL ME, DEAR Mr. Edgehill... the other night you mentioned some large insurance policy which, under certain conditions, you said might be of benefit to Mrs. Edgehill. My business is wholly spiritual and I am ignorant of all such mundane matters, but is it not possible to borrow money on it? Enough, perhaps, together with the thirty thousand you said you might be able to raise, to approximate the sum demanded by the kidnapers?"

"I carry life insurance of a hundred and fifty thousand, if that's what you mean," said Edgehill heavily. "I took it out some years ago to make sure my wife and children would be certain of support in case anything happened to me. But the only way she could benefit by that would be through my death. All I could borrow on it would be just a few thousand—not enough to make a difference."

"I see," said The Parson meekly. "I didn't know. It was merely a desperate suggestion."

"By God!" Edgehill stared at him, his face filling with a feverish light. "Perhaps you *have* suggested something!"

The Parson brightened, surprised and pleased. "Indeed! How I should rejoice if that were so! Will you explain, dear Mr. Edgehill?"

"If I die," said Edgehill slowly, "my wife gets the insurance—the full amount of the ransom! And the suicide clause in the policy has long been void!"

"Suicide!" The Parson stiffened in his chair.

Edgehill glared at him in the frenzy of his new emotion. "It's a question of my wife's life or my own, isn't it? Can you deny it? Don't be a superstitious fool!"

The Parson wrung his hands. "Perhaps not, Mr. Edgehill," he quavered. "But even so—suicide? I could not advise it! I must forbid the very thought of it!"

"Forbid and be damned!" retorted Edgehill bitterly. "You're inconsistent as well. Isn't there something even in your Bible about dying for one's friends—"

" 'Greater love hath no man than this, that a man lay down his life for his friends,'" quoted The Parson glibly. "But—"

"But how about a man's wife?" demanded Edgehill fiercely. "The mother of his children, the heart in his body? Am I to sacrifice *her* life for my own, which could only be a hell of misery forever after? That's what it comes to, isn't it? Or can you suggest any other equally certain way of rescuing her, Mr. Acton?"

"Your two little children," ventured The Parson. "Think of them, I pray you."

"They're still very, young. They need their mother most," returned their father, his face like stone. "Listen, Mr. Acton! I sent to you the other day for aid in this great trouble, and you professed anxiety to be of service. I trusted you then… I trust you now, though it seems you can't help me in the way I had hoped. But are you still willing to be of all possible assistance to Mrs. Edgehill?"

"What can I possibly answer but yes?" pleaded The Parson. "Only don't ask me to condone—"

"It was your own suggestion, even if you didn't mean it as such!" Edgehill said coldly. "And suicide seems to offer the only way out. So whether you like it or not, I shall be eternally grateful for it. *Eternally!*" he repeated with a strange smile. "But I won't hold you or name you as responsible for it, if that's what's troubling you."

The Parson decided he had gone far enough in one direction. "I am obliged to admit that I see no other way, horrible as this one is," he said, forcing a shudder. "And in spite of the fact that such an act would violate one of the strongest principles of my faith, Mr. Edgehill, I believe that it will prove you a true and noble Christian! I believe the Lord will take cognizance of the cause, and grant you His forgiveness!"

"Then I can still rely on you—afterward?"

"For everything that is in my power," surrendered The Parson.

"All right. Now for business. First, there are the children. There will be no one to look after them while Mrs. Edgehill is still absent. Her parents, whom she was going to visit when—are ill, and we have no other relatives. Besides, they should remain here—they'll be all she has when she comes back."

"I shall be most happy to take charge of them and to guard them as my own," said The Parson.

"Until Mrs. Edgehill's return. *And would you surely be able to procure that return if you could assure and deliver to her kidnapers the ransom they demand?*"

"I fully believe so. I have no doubt of it," replied The Parson with convincing sincerity.

"I am compelled to believe you. But since Mrs. Edgehill can't, some one will have to go through the necessary formalities with the Union Life Insurance Company in order to get the money with which to ransom her. It will be quite a legal problem, yet it's one I don't dare to entrust to my own lawyers. They would be too apt to insist on action that would imperil her. What could be done about that?"

"IF I DIDN'T fear to offend," ventured The Parson, "I might suggest a man I know something about through his connection with some of the unfortunates who frequent my little mission. A man who has been termed unscrupulous at times, I admit, but who is accepted as being superlatively shrewd and successful in matters of great difficulty."

"I'd take the devil himself if he could guarantee to put the thing through in time to save my wife! Who is he?"

"His name, I believe, is Mandel," said The Parson meekly.

"Henry Mandel!" Edgehill stared. "That crook! But—well, if any lawyer could get away with it, it might be Mandel. His criminal practice has made a power of him. But—why, those very fiends who have stolen my wife might be among his clients!"

"And if that were true, dear Mr. Edgehill," said The Parson boldly, "could you possibly be more certain of Mrs. Edgehill's safe return?"

Edgehill gasped. "That's true, too, I suppose! Well, I'll have to ask you to go, Mr. Acton. It will take me an hour or so to prepare the necessary instructions to leave behind—appointing you and Mandel as executors, with full power as to the insurance, changing my will and so forth… and a last letter to my wife," Edgehill said with a steady voice. Then he hesitated in embarrassment. "It's a strange thing to ask of a clergyman, Mr. Acton, but have you a gun with you? A revolver?"

The Parson gaped. "A *gun?* You mean you haven't one?"

Ten times over he cursed Sweet William, but silently. This was a contingency that had never occurred to him. Not that he didn't have a gun on his person, but to deprive himself even for a minute of the derringer strapped on a spring underneath his right sleeve was not to be thought of.

"There's nothing in the house but a shotgun out in the hall closet," said Edgehill. "However, I suppose that will do."

"A shotgun?" objected The Parson. "That's a rather awkward and uncertain way."

"All one to me," said Edgehill grimly. "I'll go down the driveway with it when I'm ready. I don't want to wake the children to such a horror. I hope someone doesn't see me leave with it."

Every variation from his original plan seemed to The Parson to offer an additional risk. Again he blasted Sweet William with a potent, silent curse. Then he thought of a way of playing safe. "I am already so committed to this terrible but necessary act of supreme self-sacrifice," he volunteered, "that I will commit myself still further. I can take the dreadful weapon with me and leave it standing behind one of the gate posts."

Edgehill looked at him suspiciously. "Are you being honest, Mr. Acton? You're not trying to trick me out of what you yourself admit is the only chance of saving Mrs. Edgehill?"

"I give you my word of honor as a Christian minister I am not," said The Parson soberly. "I am only too painfully aware that her life now depends on—yours, dear Mr. Edgehill."

At the front door Edgehill stopped The Parson to take his hand. "I'm leaving my life in trust to you, so to speak, Mr. Acton," he said huskily. "And what is far more, that of my poor beloved wife! If you should fail me—"

The Parson raised his hand toward heaven. "May God do so unto me and more also," he protested solemnly, "if I do not keep the faith!"

6

THE SHOT ON THE DRIVEWAY

THE PARSON HAD done Sweet William a grave injustice by accusing him of neglect in not keeping his appointment at the Edgehill house. Willie even had arrived there in advance of the time set. That he was in no condition to greet The Parson was no fault of Willie's. Even had he been able to act if called upon, he had sufficient company with him to prevent such compliance.

He had been taken on the previous day and driven far out of town to what his captors considered a suitable spot for the inquisition—the wagon-shed of an abandoned farmstead a mile off the main road. After a few minutes of stubborn refusal to reply to his interrogators, Willie had been turned over to Kato for an expert Japanese softening process, and in a few minutes more his hard-boiled truculence had departed from him. He answered to the very best of his ability every question put to him.

Willie confessed to all he knew about the kidnaping of Mrs. Edgehill. How Norah Weldon had selected her as a rich Royalton prospect. How Norah had notified him, and through him The Parson, of Mrs. Edgehill's intended solitary drive to Hennepin. Norah had learned this by listening in on a telephone conversation between Mrs. Edgehill and her parents.

But of the location of the hide-out where the kidnaped woman was being held to await her ransom Willie could tell nothing, even under extremest pressure. Yet he talked freely of The Parson's kidnaping operations in general, and about Henry Mandel's profitable relations with The Parson and the racket.

Willie spared nothing and nobody under the inquisitional probe of Captain Vindex and that expert lawyer, Edwin Thrale—and under the occasional ministrations of Kato. Finally he fainted.

Kato glared down at the doomed gangster. To Kato, every man in any way connected with the snatch racket was, by proxy, at least, one of those unknown fiends who had stolen and murdered two children—children Kato had loved with a devotion only less than that of Captain Vindex, their father, himself. To Kato the slaying of a kidnaper was a rite, an offering figuratively laid to those unknown little graves. Kato only waited for Captain Vindex to give the order.

But Captain Vindex was still unsatisfied. "Can you bring him to so that he can speak, Doctor?" he demanded.

Ellsworth knelt down beside Willie with his small emergency case and soon revived him.

"What was the Edgehill ransom?" demanded Captain Vindex.

"Hundred an' fifty grand," wheezed Willie. "It—it's his life insurance—'s all he's got. He—passes in his—checks tonight."

"What's that? You mean Mr. Edgehill is to be killed

tonight for the sake of getting his life insurance for the ransom?"

"If—if he don't—kill himself," Willie groaned. "Parson said he would, but I was to be there—to make sure."

"You live another day," said Captain Vindex grimly.

It was already dawn. During the day, thanks to the care he got, Willie recuperated until he was almost himself again. But with Kato hovering over him like a hawk over a chicken yard he gave the fullest details of The Parson's plans for the evening at Edgehill's home.

Half an hour before The Parson was due to arrive, the little party, including Sweet William, was concealed in the shrubbery near the house awaiting his arrival. Kato eyed Willie ominously.

"Parson come, this man make holler, Parson shoot or run away," he said to Captain Vindex. "Better I fix so can't do, you say so? Not kill, not hurt—jus' fix so can see, can walk, but not can talk or think. Just obey order like good small child. You say?"

"You can do *that?*" Dr. Ellsworth stared.

Kato bowed, hissing and smiling. "Can do. Good Japanese trick like jujutsu kind. Are Japanese secret made on nerves."

"Go to it," nodded Captain Vindex.

THE FRIGHTENED WILLIE started a scream, but Kato jumped him like a tiger, throttling it. Then with his other hand he searched out certain sensory nerves in the struggling gangster's upper body, thumbing them with a strange and special pressure. In a minute he let his victim go. Willie stood there trembling still, but with his whole expression changed. He looked dully at nothing and seemed to feel nothing, Kato bowed and smiled and hissed again in the dark.

"No make any trouble now for two-three hour. Could shoot an' wouldn't make holler. Wouldn't care."

"Good God!" breathed Dr. Ellsworth, staring at the automaton.

They saw The Parson come stealing up the driveway and watched his entrance into the house. The library was lighted up. Captain Vindex went to a window and peered in. Then he tried the door. Left secretly unlatched by The Parson's stealthy fingers for his henchman's entrance, as Willie had said it would be, it opened. Captain Vindex beckoned to the others.

For half an hour Willie and a quartet of his captors waited in a dark living room across the hall from the library, while Captain Vindex listened at the library door. When The Parson at last came out he stepped back under the shadow of the stairway. They all heard The Parson's final oath of loyalty as he departed with the shotgun.

When Edgehill went back into the library he left its door half open. There was no more reason for secrecy indoors. And for a long hour the man across the hall could see his pen traveling over paper—could watch the devouring agony grow upon his face as he wrote the arrangements for his wife's safety and bade her farewell.

Finally he finished his task and looked up—to see five men standing in a silent semicircle at the end of the room. From above handkerchiefs drawn across four of the faces steadfast eyes regarded him. The fifth man was unmasked, but he seemed to stare vacantly, as though paralyzed.

Albert Edgehill was utterly dumfounded. So absorbed

had he been that he had heard nothing, seen nothing as they moved into the room.

As he still sat stunned by the multiple apparition a sixth man entered the library from the hall, Oriental eyes gleaming above the handkerchief that crossed his face.

"I snake down on grass under trees. He still waiting behind big tree with shootgun little way this side of gate," whispered Kato. "He swear at himself hard like sailor. I think he tired of waiting."

Captain Vindex nodded.

"That's what I figured," he said half aloud.

The sound of the words broke the spell that bound Edgehill's dazed mind. He sprang to his feet, instantly certain that these were his wife's kidnapers come back—perhaps for his children! The wild thought was the natural product of his long torment. They were between him and the door, and his only weapon was gone. Mr. Acton had carried it away!

"Oh, my God!" he groaned. "Leave them alone! Haven't you done enough to me?"

"They?" answered Captain Vindex's deep voice. "Oh, the children! It's you we want. Take him."

In a second Edgehill was seized and gagged, although without brutality. "Kidnaping—me—too?" he managed to strain through the handkerchief before it was wholly stuffed into his mouth.

"Yes, you too," said Captain Vindex. "Kato, see if you can find his bedroom upstairs. Bring down another suit of clothes, underwear, everything!" He added, in a mutter as though speaking to himself, "They're about the same size… same sort of hair… even their faces are more or less the same shape… Mr. Edgehill," Vindex ordered aloud, "strip to the buff. Unless you want it done for you!"

Edgehill stared pop-eyed at this amazing order. Madman! But he began to undress to avoid having his clothes torn off of him. When Kato returned from his errand Edgehill was as naked, except for the cloth that bound the gag in place. *But so was one other man*—the man who had not been masked with a handkerchief, and who was still gazing idiotically at nothing across the room. He too had been told to strip, and he had obeyed without a word and without hesitation.

Both were ordered to dress, Edgehill in the clothes brought down by Kato, Willie in those discarded by Edgehill. Kato bundled Willie's discards into his shirt and tied them up. Then Edgehill was turned into a cocoon with wrappings wound and bound about him, so that he could neither see nor hear, and left lying on the floor of his own library.

Kato steered Willie out into the hall.

"There's a hat! Put that on him and pull it down," bade Captain Vindex. He put the light out before reopening the front door and Willie was headed down the driveway. Kato followed him, under the deeper shadow of the trees.

FROM BEHIND THE trunk of a big oak standing thirty feet inside the gate, The Parson watched his victim come plodding heavily down the gravel road, his head bowed, his hands hanging helplessly, hopelessly at his sides. He walked through the darkness with the air of a man going to his execution, but he came steadily onward toward the big stone gateposts looming against a faintly star-lit sky.

"Here comes the true and noble Christian," grinned

The Parson to himself. "The simple-minded suicide for the wife's sweet sake—and for mine! Well, dear Mr. Edgehill, we'll take that curse off your soul, anyway—and may it do you a lot of good up there!"

And as the plodding figure reached the tree behind which he was hidden, he stepped quickly out, thrust the muzzle up under its chin and pulled the trigger. Instantly he dropped the shotgun onto the driveway and darted back behind the oak, brushing his black cotton gloves together.

The shot sounded like a cannon in the stillness of the night. The Parson more than half expected to see lights begin to blaze out all over the house as he stared back up the driveway. Or to hear distant sounds indicating that other homes had been aroused.

But no lights appeared, no sounds made themselves evident from any direction. For full five minutes he waited motionless, prepared to steal diagonally across the lawn in the darkness and drop over the wall into the street as opportunity offered.

At last, his sharp eyes and sharper ears certifying that no interruption was on the way, he ventured to steal out from his hiding place and bend over the body with a tiny flashlight, shaded with his hand. He turned from what had been the head with a disgusted "Faugh!"

But the clothes, the watch chain, the heavy seal ring on the left third finger, all promised easy and unquestionable identification. The right hand was tightly closed over some small object that he couldn't see. He ventured to pry the fingers open enough to look at it. It was a little ivory miniature of Mrs. Edgehill, which had been standing on Edgehill's desk in the library.

All in all, together with the incontestable documentary evidence he knew would be in the house, the most complete proof of suicide that could possibly be offered! No one would question it.

The Parson grinned again, as he slipped through the shadows, out of the gate and down two long blocks occupied only by private estates—still unlighted—to the distant corner around which he had parked his car.

7

THE MOUTHPIECE

THE DEATH OF Albert Edgehill, prominent resident of Royalton and supposedly a millionaire, would have been worth at least two sticks and a single-column cut in the Chicago papers in any event.

But the discovery of his body, faceless but recognizable by its clothing, and the disclosure of his brave and ghastly self-sacrifice, with all the sensational trimmings of the hitherto suppressed kidnaping of his wife, which were revealed to newspapermen by the instructions written just before he blew his head off, put him on the first page with a bang.

One of the main features of the news was the startling appointment by Mr. Edgehill, just before his suicide, of the Reverend Reuben Acton and the notorious Henry Mandel as the suicide's authorized representatives to collect his life insurance and apply it, in default of other sufficient funds, to the ransom of Mrs. Edgehill.

But it was recalled, not without some invidious comment, that the almost unknown pastor of the little South Side Christian Mission had twice before figured in negotiations between kidnapers and the families of their victims. It was also suggested that such a novel proce-

dure as the collection and
application of Edgehill's
life insurance for use as
ransom money was possi-
bly extra-legal.

Yet no one ventured to
condemn it outright, or
to take steps to prevent
its execution, since it was
obvious that Mrs. Edge-
hill's life might depend
on it. It was also admit-
ted that if any lawyer

Captain Vindex

could put such a thing over, it was Mandel. Late papers
announced that the Union Life and Accident Company
had agreed to cooperate.

That was the situation faced by Captain Vindex and his
associates thirty-six hours after they had saved Edgehill
and sent Sweet William to be murdered in his place.

"The Parson's put another one over on us!" Burns
growled. "All we've done so far is to put good money in
his pocket!"

"How do you make that out?" asked Thrale.

"Haven't we just paid off Willie, King of Hearts for
him? Not countin' in poor Norah Weldon? He don't have
to split with them now, does he?"

"He hasn't even got his own yet," said Captain Vindex.

"Why not? He's got the whole of it—or will have. Don't
the papers say the company's goin' to turn the check over
today? To be paid to the kidnapers?"

"But even so, it will take several days more to turn it into cash for division. A job, by the way, which The Parson, as a poor missionary and as a man under the limelight besides, would have to leave to some one else."

"To Mandel, of course," put in Thrale. "Being legal protector, political go-between and business manager to The Parson and the racket, as Willie confided to us, he'd be the brother who turns hot money into cold."

"Yeah," Burns gritted, "but when this thing breaks wide open, as it's bound to sooner or later, what happens next? Even if we *have* turned kidnapers like The Parson, with a hideout an' all, we can't hold Edgehill forever, can we? I don't see even yet why we had to kidnap him, Captain Vindex."

"It was a situation we were forced into. When Willie told us what was due to happen that night we had to save his life for him, didn't we?"

"Why couldn't we simply have killed off The Parson when he came?" asked Dr. Ellsworth. "We knew he was there on an errand of murder!"

"Yes, but we knew also what would happen to Mrs. Edgehill if The Parson's next regular call wasn't received on time at the hide-out. Shooting him would have meant putting a bullet into her heart—or worse. If Willie's information about that hellish safeguard of his was to be trusted."

"It was, all right," asserted Burns glumly.

"As far as Edgehill's concerned, he'll have to stay put till we get hold of his wife," Vindex explained. "What else could we have done with him? Left him alone to kill himself? If he hadn't done it The Parson would certainly have finished the job. Or if we'd gone off and left him after The Parson had killed Willie, Edgehill would have shown himself and the same result would have followed. He couldn't have been trusted. Or, again, if the insurance money had escaped The Parson, Mrs. Edgehill's life would have paid for it. As it is, The Parson believes that he did kill Edgehill. So as long as Edgehill is kept under cover Mrs. Edgehill is probably safe—until we can find her."

"Even then," Thrale shook his head, "there'll be trouble enough about the insurance when Edgehill does show up alive, and The Parson may take it out on both of them. He and Mandel will have a lot of explaining to do!"

"Yeah," said Burns, "but I'll bet Edgehill got the surprise of his life when he found he'd been kidnaped into a swell apartment out in Oak Park with all the comforts of home, includin' a Jap valet as good as Kato. Everything excep' the daily paper an' a phone an' a key to the front door! But as Thrale says, he can't stay there for life. So what?"

"THERE'S ONLY ONE answer," said Captain Vindex. "We've got to recover both the woman and the money. And the children. But they're safe enough somewhere. It's a matter of public knowledge that Edgehill entrusted the children to The Parson, so he'd have to restore them."

"Yes, that's all we got to do," said Burns dryly. "An' we haven't been half trying. So let's get started."

"All right. Then see if you can get Mandel on the phone for me. Try his office."

Burns stared. "Mandel! An' who the hell shall I say is callin'?"

Captain Vindex grinned briefly. "Tell him that Mr. Acton—the Reverend Reuben Acton—would like to speak with him on a most important matter."

Burns shook his head. But he put in the call, however, and in a minute handed over the instrument.

Captain Vindex cleared his throat. "Mr. Mandel? This is Mr. Acton on the phone," he said in The Parson's voice, lightly stressing the last three words. "So sorry to bother you, but something has come up… Oh, no, something quite personal concerning the welfare of a pair of my proteges here at the mission… No, tomorrow won't do, unfortunately. They might be picked up at any time. You'd oblige me by seeing us this evening… What? Oh, my Friday evening prayer meeting… I'll arrange for that…."

Mandel evidently made further objection, for Captain Vindex's expression changed as subtly as that of The Parson himself might have done. His voice, also, became oilier; but with a faint tincture of poison in it. "Ah? Then let me remind you of King Solomon's words, dear Mr. Mandel. 'Because I have called and ye refused… I also will laugh at your calamity; I will mock when your fear cometh.' See Proverbs One, Verses Twenty-four and six… What? Oh, very well, at a little after six. Thank you, dear Mr. Mandel!"

Burns whistled in open admiration. "You put it over!"

"Yes," said Captain Vindex. "Mr. Mandel will receive The Parson and some of his underlings, supposedly in trouble, a few minutes after six at his office in the Loop. We're to enter through the basement and go up in the freight elevator, just to avoid all unkind suspicion at this present time. He'll arrange it. But he didn't like it, although he obeyed orders. Showing where The Parson stands with him."

"Well, the voice sounded perfect," said Burns soberly. "But you think the rest will come as easy? You never seen

The Parson except disguised or in the dark, Captain Vindex, an' them two devils would be pretty well acquainted."

"I never forget a voice. And you will remember that when I first heard The Parson's voice I believed it was going to be the last thing I was to hear on earth. And as for the rest of it," shrugged Captain Vindex, "there's really nothing but these newspaper cuts to go on, of course. Yet I think I can get us inside his office."

HENRY MANDEL IN person, wearing patent leathers and diamonds, opened his outer office at six-ten that evening, after first suspiciously investigating his visitors through a crack. The empty marble corridor was dusky, the lights having been turned out.

Inside it was even darker, the shade having been drawn on every window. Mr. Mandel viewed Captain Vindex's tough following with evident disfavor—a feeling from which he hastened to disassociate the Reverend Reuben Acton.

"These dumb gunnies!" he said. " 'F it wasn't for you, Mr. Acton, I'd let 'em take their chances. 'S more money in it anyway, once they get in jail!"

"Out of my pocket," said the fake Mr. Acton dryly. "They're my boys, Henry, and I want you to treat them right. They're good boys."

"Oh, sure, sure! Don't I always look after them boys of yours, Parson? But listen, you got a cold or a bum throat or something. Come, I'll give you some fine old Three Star Hennessey I got in my private safe. Let these bums wait outside a minute."

Mandel led the way through a pair of empty and dusky rooms into his private office, closing its door on his prospective clients. The window was already darkened by a heavy drape, and he shaded even his desk light. "No need advertising I do a business here after office hours," he explained. "The papers seem to want to rub it into us account of that Edgehill business already, Parson."

He opened his private safe, took out a bottle and two glasses, and poured the drinks. "Well, anyhow, here's to the *selig* Mr. Edgehill, at nine dollars a quart," he toasted. "Unless he is taking the credit that belongs to someone else," he added with a sharp, sly look at his companion.

The "Reverend Reuben Acton," his face in shadow, couldn't be seen to turn a hair at the cryptic hint of murder. "You can afford it, Henry," he said dryly. "How soon are you going to be able to cash that check?" But he held his breath as he waited for the answer.

"Oi, business, always business with you, Parson," chuckled Mandel. "No time for a little joke. Well, right away I promise you. It's pretty big, a hunderd and fifty grand. But I got a bank in Detroit that can handle it quick and quiet. Maybe we better not stir up the criminals any more here in Chicago, Parson. Although it ain't hot—it's good, clean, honest money that nobody need be ashamed of, ain't it?"

Captain Vindex had his first answer.

"It's in the safe?"

"Sure it's in the safe! In *this* safe, not the office safe. You needn't worry! 'S my own private safe, and nobody's got the combination but me. Well, Parson, have another little drink, then I get at those bad boys of yours. What've they been doing? No snatch business, I hope! Let the papers get the bad taste out of their mouth again first!"

He poured out two more full glasses, tossing his own off at once.

"No snatch business? That depends," said the "Reverend Reuben Acton" somberly. "Where are the Edgehill children? Are they safe?"

Mandel was startled by that extraordinary question, "Where?" he stared. "Where would they be except out in Cicero with that Brennan woman, where we put them! And what do you mean, safe, Mr. Acton? That Lulu Brennan wouldn't dare to cross me. Like I told you, I got a till-robbing on her. But—"

"We're going out there to get them," snapped The Parson, standing up. "So come!"

MANDEL'S FACE OPENED wide, at the same time losing a little color. His popping eyes saw less than actuality, however, because he was mentally envisioning another prospect that greatly alarmed him.

"Listen, Mr. Acton," he stammered, "I hope you ain't got any foolish idea of taking those children anywheres to cash in on. If you have, I wash my hands of it right here and now! I wouldn't have nothing to do with it, nor I couldn't get you out of it, either! My God, don't everybody know Edgehill left you the care of them till we got his own wife back? So you've got to hand them over safe and sound and for nothing! You've *got* to! And *me* go with you on such a business? Are you crazy? I'm a lawyer. I ain't in the kidnaping business!"

"The Parson" backed to the door and threw it open.

"Come," he repeated harshly to the lawyer as his three tough-looking followers filed in. "And first give me that check out of the safe!"

"But thirty thousand of it's mine! You act like I was trying to do you out of it! What is it, a frame or a holdup?"

Burns grinned at him. "Damned if it doesn't look like another snatch, to me!" he jeered.

"I said the check!" barked Captain Vindex.

Mandel dug it out of a drawer with trembling fingers.

"And now," said "The Parson," pocketing the check, "Mr. Mandel is going with us to Cicero to get the Edgehill children. After that—"

"Don't—aren't you forgetting your prayer meeting, Parson?" babbled Mandel in a pathetic attempt at propitiation.

"—After that he's going to help us find Mrs. Edgehill herself. He says she's here in the city."

Mandel groaned in despair, hardly daring to look at the speaker. The Parson was crazy! He must have gone insane! He would be twice as dangerous as ever....

Thanks to the precautions he himself had taken to insure a wholly private and unwitnessed interview, Mandel was led out of the big building by the freight elevator and the rear exit without even a chance of rescue, to be settled in the rear seat of a sedan standing in the back alley. One of The Parson's punks with a gun was on each side of him. Vindex himself took the wheel.

8

THE PARSON'S DEN

SET AMID A row of tenements was a larger building with a wider front, divided into two unequal parts, each section having its own entrance from the sidewalk. The nearer entrance was marked *office*. This door led into a dark hall, off which a dingy front room opened on the right hand side to justify the sign on the outer door. Beyond a stairway in the hall interior swinging doors opened into a smelly soup-and-slum kitchen.

The entrance to the wider section consisted of a pair of double doors. The floor had been planned originally as a saloon and dance hall. Now, by the simple substitution of rows of benches for beer-stained tables, and by placing a combination pulpit-harmonium on the old orchestra platform, it had been converted into the chapel of what stood advertised across the front of the entire building as:

THE SOUTH SIDE CHRISTIAN MISSION
Rev. Reuben Acton, Pastor

The second story on the office side was occupied by a pool room, a reading room in which most of the reading was done from the faces of playing cards, and, at the rear, by The Parson's own private study.

Above these and throughout the two stories above the chapel, all floors were cut up into flops graded from free to thirty-five cents for the price of a night's lodging, as advertised by a ratecard in the hall.

In the rear the mission appeared to back up against the end of a closed brick warehouse. The construction that united the two buildings seemed, from the inside of each, to be nothing but a solid end wall. Yet it covered and included what had been, and still showed on the city's real estate maps, as an end-to-end pair of ten-foot back yards.

This improvement had been quietly put in by The Parson himself for purposes of his own, without bothering the building department either for permit or inspection. As deceptive from all sides as a blank wall—unless discovered by accurate inside measurements of both buildings—it had as many connections with the underworld as a subway station; although they were blinder.

It also contained rooms and passages far more secure against invasion than those of the two less substantial structures it so illegitimately connected and enlarged. It was proof against almost anything short of dynamite.

Ordinarily an air of surreptitious detachment existed about both the South Side Christian Mission and the street on which it stood. As if each were something to slip into or out of, while pretending to be going somewhere else.

But on the Friday evening following the excitement of the Edgehill suicide, things were different. Not only did the public advertisement of the Reverend Reuben

Acton attract curiosity-seekers from other parts of town, but Alderman McGonnigle, who owned the barroom on the corner, had seized upon the opportunity for a little public demonstration.

So that the real Reverend Reuben Acton, prepared for nothing more than one of his regular stock-in-trade Friday night prayer meetings, and never less inclined to stand in the glare of the limelight, was astonished to find himself the object and the center of a gathering that filled the chapel. There were even floral decorations.

And to his increased discomfort he noted that his audience contained another alderman from city hall besides McGonnigle, plus a deputy city clerk and several reporters. Three uptown clergymen in buttoned frock coats helped to occupy the front seats, together with the political and journalistic contingents. All were present to express their sense of Christian brotherhood in the doing of good works. His own people, his punks from the more practical quarter of the mission, and the usual loafers and drifters in from the streets, were there in force; yet in a minority.

Mr. McGonnigle sidetracked the prayer meeting after The Parson's slightly confused opening invocation by the simple method of mounting the platform and undoing his mouth.

"LADIES AN' GENTS," orated Alderman McGonnigle, "there's no needcessity of me introdjucin' to you the man known like a father an' a mother to ever'body in this grand an' glorious Ward of which I have the honor to repersent in this fair city—the man who in this noble mission we are now in rescues the perishin' from sin an' feeds the hungary, body an' soul. You have jus' heard him prayin' for you, an' you seen his pitchers in the paper. So I make the motion that the Reverend Reuben Acton favor us with how he contacted them crool snatchers of our sacred American homes an' persuaded them to accep' ransom for the poor woman they was holdin' in endurance vile, but who we can now hope with pleasure to see back in our midst! All in favor of the motion will please raise their right hand."

They didn't raise it, but they used it for the loudest kind of clapping, thus proving that Alderman McGonnigle had struck a popular cord. The Reverend Reuben Acton could have murdered him on the spot, not in cold blood, but very cheerfully.

Yet he was constrained to adapt himself to the embarrassing circumstances. With a bow to his introducer and an oily smile he stepped forward.

"My beloved friends," began The Parson in a soft and mealy voice, although his half-veiled eyes were bloodshot with fury, "dear Alderman McGonnigle's tongue has dripped honey on which I feel myself and my conscience wholly unworthy to feed—especially as we all of us know that poor Mrs. Edgehill is still in the hands of those who so cruelly tore her from her happy home, the ransom transaction not yet having been entirely completed. Nevertheless, I may say I am sure that, as Alderman McGonnigle has already stated, we have good reason to hope she will very soon again be with us.

"And yet," went on The Parson, warming to his subject, "what grief awaits that poor lady when she returns only to find that her brave, true-hearted husband chose to die that she might be saved! That in humble imitation of Our

Lord—see First Timothy, Two, Six—Albert Edgehill 'gave himself a ransom for—'"

Almost at the mention of the name The Parson's eyes fell on the face of the man he named—*Albert Edgehill!*

He stopped as if struck by lightning. On the last bench, near the door, sat Albert Edgehill, plain and unmistakable, staring back at him!

Up to that instant The Parson had been certain that Albert Edgehill lay dead and buried in a suicide's grave. Hadn't he attended to the matter himself, and with his usual thoroughness? Nor did he believe in the return of the dead. His long experience, as well as his cold common sense, forbade it. So he immediately realized that the man whose head he had blown off on the Edgehill driveway in the dark could not have been Edgehill.

Therefore, Edgehill had put something over on him. Edgehill had sent another man to death. And, since, two and two make four, that other man must have been the missing William, King of Hearts!

But that wasn't the worst of it. Edgehill, by remaining alive, had turned the ransom check for a hundred and fifty thousand, now at Mandel's office, into a worthless scrap of paper. And there would inevitably be prompt and distressing investigation into the questions of the identity of the suicide of the dead man, as well as regarding the payment and the further disposition of Edgehill's life insurance!

That would be *too* much! Edgehill had no *right* to be alive!

The Parson's audience, sensing from his sudden breaking off in the middle of a sentence and from the startling change in his appearance that something extraordinary was occurring, had frozen. It could have heard a pin drop. **ALL AT ONCE** The Parson's tension broke. His face turned into that of a devil. His right hand shot straight toward Edgehill. His sleevegun leaped into it. Fire and smoke burst from the gun.

Not even stopping to see whether he had hit or missed, The Parson turned and leaped across the stage. He pressed a button in the frame of a picture. A solid block of the wall opened—long enough to let him dive through. Then it swung back into place with a dull thud. So solid was this secret and long-prepared getaway that The Parson couldn't even hear the turmoil he had left behind him. Shrieks, yells and curses filled the chapel. Men and women went down by dozens to be kicked and trampled in the rush to get out. Edgehill was unharmed.

The Parson knew that he had burned his ships behind him; that as the Reverend Reuben Acton, pastor of the South Side Christian Mission in Chicago, he was through. But he also knew that in all probability he had only briefly anticipated his finish. The inquiries threatened by Edgehill's unexpected resurrection would in any case have finally resulted in exposure. Besides which, he had been getting an uneasy feeling that his merciless enemy, Captain Vindex, was somehow too close to him or knew too much. And in that case a change in his assumed character and in his headquarters was practically called for.

First, however, he would take his revenge! If he wasn't to get that hundred and fifty grand, at least he still had Mrs. Edgehill!

After collecting some papers from the desk in his study

in the other side of the mission he'd attend to her—and take his time about it. It would take the police hours to break into his private fortress between the mission and the warehouse. It would be like breaking into a modern bank safe, unless they knew how.

Yes, and there were still the Edgehill children tucked away in Cicero. Only he and Mandel knew where. Edgehill would wish he *had* died when he got *all* the news! After finishing with the woman, The Parson meant to get hold of Mandel. There might be some wreckage from that check even yet, if Henry could act fast enough in the morning.

The Parson hurried through a narrow passage walled with stone, plunged up some iron stairs, and halted before the mechanism of bars and bolts that opened the way into his study in the other section of the mission. He touched a lever and the wall opened half an inch. Nor was there any sound from the inside.

He pressed the lever and a square of wall swung wide to let him step through it. To his amazement, on a chair in the center of the study sat Mandel, grinning at him.

The Parson staggered and clutched at his desk. For the grin on that fat face was rigid, bloodless, horrible. And Henry Mandel neither spoke nor moved nor saw, although his eyes, bulging in their sockets, seemed to be staring straight at the Reverend Reuben Acton.

On Mr. Mandel's white forehead glowed a freshly branded V.

9

THE BRAND ON MANDEL'S FOREHEAD

CAPTAIN VINDEX, A little earlier that Friday evening, was feeling like a man who has fallen off a dock, and comes up with a pearl in each hand. Until he entered Mandel's office he hadn't realized the full extent of the crooked criminal lawyer's connection with the Edgehill snatch. But now he had Edgehill's life insurance check in his pocket. He was in the auto on his way to get Edgehill's children and restore them. And he even had hopes of being able to extract from Mr. Mandel some amplification of the latter's hint that Mrs. Edgehill herself was held in a hideout right in the city of Chicago.

Meanwhile, even allowing for the psychology of prepared expectance, plus the effect of his own lucky shots at intimate details of the Edgehill case presumably known solely to The Parson, Captain Vindex could only regard as a miracle the persistence of the lawyer's illusion that he was the Reverend Acton.

But he had not made allowance for the fact that Mandel's ordinarily brilliant powers of perception were paralyzed by the predicament in which he found himself. Nor for the lawyer's blind and not unreasonable panic at what he took for the proposal to kidnap the Edgehill children—an act for which the legal mind foresaw terrible and inevitable consequences.

Mandel's panic was increased when he was forced to accompany The Parson to the very door of the cheap apartment in Cicero and demand the children from the Brennan woman, who knew him only too well. He felt as if he were strapping himself into the electric chair by that single transaction.

But it was Captain Vindex who bore the children out to the car. It was Captain Vindex who gathered them tenderly into his arms in the back seat, while Mandel took a place in front beside the new driver, a gun-muzzle firmly pressed against his spine between his shoulder blades.

Mandel's first doubt concerning The Parson's actual identity came some fifteen minutes later, when he caught a glimpse in the rear-view mirror of the two little golden heads resting peacefully against The Parson's shoulders, while The Parson's arms enwrapped the two small bodies and The Parson's face looked down upon them with a look that was terrible in its intensity, terrible in its expression of agony—and of love.

But Mandel's doubt was purely academic. It simply seemed impossible to him that such an expression could ever lie on the face of the Reverend Reuben Acton. He was unquestionably mistaken in his first involuntary interpretation of the look!

If he had known it, he had made no mistake. Captain Vindex was on the rack of memory. He was undergoing exquisite torture at the feeling of those little bodies in his arms, at the warm scent of their golden hair, at the sleepy and contented prattle that stabbed him to the heart, word by word. He was reliving the past with his own children—children long in their unknown graves after unknown horrors at the hands of such men as the Reverend Reuben Acton and his equally criminal lawyer, Henry Mandel!

Mandel's panic was enhanced when the car stopped in front of an apartment house in Oak Park, into which the Reverend Reuben Acton calmly carried the children. So, Mandel thought, The Parson had already had a fresh hideout prepared for them when he came to the office! Mandel ventured a glance at the door, but was harshly directed to keep his eyes in front.

Some ages later, it seemed to him, The Parson returned to the sedan, accompanied by two other men. The driver received orders to get back into the city as quickly as possible.

It was dark when Mandel was hustled out of the car and through a doorway that looked like the entrance to a tenement. But he had caught a glimpse of the front of the building and of a sign above it. So that he rightly judged he was in the Reverend Reuben Acton's South Side Christian Mission—a place Mr. Mandel had always kept far away from.

The door and windows of the chapel, a few yards farther down the sidewalk, were emitting both light and the droning sound of speech. But only two of the seven men the car had held moved on to visit the prayer meeting. The Parson himself, and three others, accompanied Mandel into the study. A dapper-looking punk jerked his feet down from a desk and stood up to stare at them, particularly at the Reverend Reuben Acton.

"Anybody here?" snapped the false Parson.

"WHAT—WHAT THE HELL, ain't you *there*, boss?" gaped the punk. "What you mean, anybody here? There's just me, an' Moxie out back somewheres. All the rest's in the chapel listenin' to *you!*"

"Look up Moxie!" commanded "The Parson." Two of his companions immediately vanished to obey the order. "You!" he barked at the gaping punk, "Upstairs!"

They trailed him to the top of the house and across and above the chapel. The punk was in a daze, but he said nothing about it. One didn't argue with The Parson or intrude with any comment when he was in one of his black moods. After lighting and inspecting every room and every space above the first floor on both sides of the mission, they all returned to The Parson's private study. And there "The Parson" nodded at the punk.

"Take him, Kato!"

The dapper gangster, already suspicious of his chief, reached wildly for a gun. But he was knocked on the head, bound, gagged and dragged out to be dumped in a broom closet in the hall within a minute and a half. Henry Mandel watched the process in a state of reeling amazement and ominous foreboding. Then "The Parson" turned on him savagely.

"Well, if she isn't here where is she?" There was no further attempt at disguise in either Captain Vindex's voice or his manner.

What Mandel saw and heard filled his stomach with a load of ice. Suddenly even the face was different. It flamed at him, while the eyes that bored into him froze him with their look, far beyond any similar effect he had ever noted as a result of The Parson's most murderous fury.

"Great God!" he whispered. "You—you ain't Acton! You *ain't* The Parson! Who are you?"

Captain Vindex barely opened his lips. "Death at once—unless you answer!"

Henry Mandel, before whose bullying sarcasm witnesses withered and forgot their lines—Henry Mandel, so famous for his legal adroitness, for his overbearing court room brutality and for his criminal wealth, trembled and whined, only too eager to oblige.

"You mean Mrs. Edgehill? So help me, if she ain't here, I don't know."

"You said she was here—in the city! You said—"

"Is that cross-examination?" interrupted Mandel, tossing both hands so that his rings glittered. "Wait one minute and please listen! I know what I said. I said you—I mean The Parson—had her safe here in the city, yes! But is this place *all* the city? All I know is that he told me she was somewhere in the city! Some things Mr. Acton wouldn't tell anybody. And I wouldn't let him, would I? The less I know about some things, the better—and that's the truth!"

The lawyer's painful anxiety was patent. And, unhappily, so was the sincerity of his protest.

Captain Vindex frowned.

"Well, he's judged already, isn't he?" suggested Dr. Ellsworth in his gentle voice. Long, nervous fingers writhed in their peculiar reaction to his emotion whenever the loss of his own children was recalled to him.

"Yeah, to the tune of thirty thousand dollars out o' that blood money!" rumbled Burns fiercely. "We all heard 'im!

He's fully as bad as them that took her an' may be torturin'
her this moment! Worse, if you ask me, because he plays
safe behind the scenes an' sucks some o' the blood he ain't
got the nerve to spill himself!"

Kato contented himself with waiting, his tigerish eyes
alternating between the figure of his hoped-for prey and
Captain Vindex.

MANDEL DISTINCTLY FELT the hand of death finger-
ing him. And suddenly he reacted with the courage of a
cornered rat. With a surprisingly swift motion for a fat
man he dived to the floor for the gun dropped by the punk
whom Kato had subdued, seized it, rolled up on to his
knees and fired.

He wasn't quite quick enough, though he had his chance
to shoot. Two shots rang out together so closely that it
would have been hard to say which was fired first. It would
not have been hard to say which was fired the straightest.

Mandel's bones seemed to turn to rubber inside his flesh.
The fat rolls in his fat face, set plump upon his fat shoulders, began to dissolve. He flattened to the floor like a
punctured toy balloon. He had been shot directly through
the heart.

Captain Vindex stared at him as he waved the smoke
out of his automatic.

"Pick him up and prop him in a chair," he said at last.
"This is The Parson's office, and he may return to it before
we have a chance or a reason to prevent him. We'll leave
him a visitor who may interest him."

"Oh, good!" said Kato, as he lifted the great bulk and
began stuffing it into position with cushions from the
couch. "And you put same beautiful perscription on fore-

head you put on telephone lady? Like we leave on seven in New York when we save little small Perham child from Parson? And need five more to make even because this man make only two."

"Sweet William, King of Hearts?" suggested Burns, with a dry look at Kato.

Kato shook his head. "No good. Had no head left to put perscription, so that no count," he said sternly. "Should have done before."

"Hell's bells!" Burns murmured, with a grim smile. "We'll have to land some more of them to keep in Kato's good graces."

"And to prevent or punish as many more horrors of the kind as we can," said Captain Vindex, as he proceeded to impress the Sign of Vengeance. "Kato may soon be able to enlarge his record. We haven't got on the track of Mrs. Edgehill yet! And when we do anything may happen."

"Oh, good!" said Kato. "I help!"

Feet clattered up the wooden stairs and down the hall. Thrale, who had gone with Albert Edgehill to The Parson's prayer meeting, according to plan, burst in through the door.

"Hell to pay at the meeting!" he announced hoarsely. "The Parson suddenly took a shot at us from the platform—in the middle of a speech—and disappeared! If we hadn't been sitting way at the back I wouldn't be here yet! They're fighting to get out!"

Ellsworth was speechless.

"Took a shot?" Burns bellowed with surprise.

"Did he get Edgehill?" Captain Vindex asked sharply.

"No? All right! I thought it might happen—that or something like it. Come!"

"Thought what might happen?" gasped Burns a minute later as all five halted near the entrance to the chapel. There was no getting in against the stream still violently struggling to get out. They had to stand aside.

"That when The Parson saw a dead man watching, he must say or do something he couldn't explain afterwards—which might give us justifiable cause for executing him," Vindex answered. "But I didn't think he'd actually try to kill Edgehill a second time in front of several hundred witnesses. How did he disappear?"

"Why, I was so startled I wasn't sure just what I did see! But several others said they saw it, too," Thrale explained. "The Parson went right through the back wall."

"Through the wall?" snapped Captain Vindex. "How—unless—my God! It's Mrs. Edgehill I may have killed!" he said suddenly. "Wait!"

Burns, Thrale, Ellsworth, Kato—and Edgehill, who had joined them—waited in breathless anxiety.

"The Parson had a secret door for his getaway—or to his hide-away—or both," Captain Vindex said slowly at last. "Yet he was rarely in the chapel, and so—of *course!* From the study there'll be another door—or an exit! Back again!" Vindex cried. "And pray it's not too late!"

10

THE TWO IN BLACK

BRACED AGAINST THE desk The Parson stared at that dreadful red brand on Mandel's forehead almost as fixedly as the unseeing eyes of Henry Mandel stared at himself. No mere corpse could disturb The Parson. But this corpse, partly because of its utter unexpectedness, hit him quite as hard as the sight of another man, alive, had done, a bare three minutes earlier. The sight of a man alive who should have been even deader than Mandel.

And what a hideously accurate coincidence! For The Parson perceived it to be true that the big lawyer could only have been dead for a bare three minutes or so before his own arrival. The red stain on the expansive flowered-satin vest was still spreading.

But Mandel, who, while living had never even let himself be seen anywhere near the mission—how did he happen to be there dead?

The answer to that, though it but added to the mystery, was written on his forehead! That ominous and bloody V spelled *Vindex!*

So he had been right after all, thought The Parson grimly. His secret enemy was not only close upon him, but was well within his next-to-last defenses! It was time indeed to retreat!

His brain filled with increased fury rather than fear. First the papers he had come for. Then to finish up with Mrs. Edgehill, that final satisfaction. And then—

He slipped the papers from a secret recess in his desk into his pocket, thinking only that there was now no possibility of saving anything from the Edgehill ransom money. Or was there?

His eyes flew back to the body. He tried to remember whether Mandel was accustomed to keep his keys steel-chained and locked about his waist.

The Parson moved over to Mandel to see whether he could borrow the keys without wasting too much time. There was a rush of feet out in the corridor and the door of the study flew open with a bang. Even then he could have made his safe escape through the aperture in the rear wall if he had acted instantly. But what he saw in front of him nailed him to the floor.

Just across the threshold, and evidently quite as startled for the moment as was The Parson himself, stood his own double. He might have been looking into a mirror—a cheap one that offered some minor distortion and disfigurement.

All in an instant The Parson knew what it meant—he knew how things had happened—he sensed his double's true identity. Just as if an incompleted picture puzzle had suddenly and miraculously put itself together.

"Captain Vindex!" The Parson snarled.

The name as it broke from his lips constituted as black a curse as he had ever uttered. And he would have followed the curse up by a mad assault on certain death, thinking only to take that enemy with him, if the face of Albert Edgehill in the background had not reminded him just in time of a vengeance almost as satisfying and far more comprehensive.

Instead of precipitating the crisis, The Parson whirled and leaped back through the opening.

Captain Vindex, with Kato beside him, was instantly at The Parson's heels. They collided as they converged on the narrow aperture. But tumbling through it they accomplished what the fleeing Parson had had no time to attend to properly. They hit against the lever, and the wall closed behind them so swiftly that their four companions were left within the study, abruptly cut off from pursuit.

Captain Vindex and Kato picked themselves up from a concrete floor to hear The Parson's running footsteps already far ahead of them.

"This place is where she is!" gasped Vindex breathlessly. "It must be! And that devil will kill her now in sheer revenge before we can stop him! Which way did he go?"

For the passage branched at a narrow mid-stair landing, and went right and left, as well as up and down. The Parson was nowhere either visible or audible. What little light there was came from a few dim electric bulbs, spaced at long intervals on an open wire strung at the angle of wall and ceiling.

"I take off shoes and snake around catfoot," whispered Kato. "You wait here. Maybe I find."

BUT CAPTAIN VINDEX had another idea. "Kato, that lighting arrangement is just amateur work. It would have to be! Probably comes through on a single wire plugged in on the mission service. That's why the bulbs are all so dim. Chances are, if we broke it they'd be in the dark all over the place. That might be Mrs. Edgehill's salvation—and ours!"

Kato hissed softly in honest admiration. "Please, you wait one minute! I add small improvement that show Japanese also smart nation for thinking!"

He scooted away in silent stocking feet to vanish around the further turn; reappearing a little later along the second passage. He had not been gone for less than the minute specified, yet Captain Vindex was on edge.

"What the devil have you been doing?" he demanded. "We've got to get busy!"

"Are busy now," said Kato proudly, showing him a large but half empty box of parlor matches. He threw a scattering handful down one flight of stairs, a second handful up the other one. "Saw box on desk of honorable Parson before we jump into dark place, and take along," he explained. "Are useful to see, but are even more good on stone floor. Have therefore sprinkle all places so when get stepped on shall make sparkle and snap. Then we see where to shoot at and others don't. You take off shoes like me. Then we break lamp string."

"My hat's off to you!" rapped Captain Vindex as he hurriedly obeyed the suggestion. "All right—now!"

He arched his back against the wall of the corridor, while Kato climbed his shoulders like a cat to seize the open light wire. In a second everything went dark, upstairs and down as well as on their own level.

They got immediate results of another nature. The sound of a door down the right hand corridor, flung angrily open;

the sound of a voice, as cold, as precise and as poisonous as the fang of a rattlesnake:

"Who did that? What damned white-livered punk pulled that switch? By God, are you yellow rats trying to desert in the dark? Answer, somebody!"

It was The Parson's voice. Captain Vindex clutched at Kato's arm. Another voice replied from the indeterminate distance and direction of invisibility: "Here, boss—it's me, Peto. Over here! Me, I never touched it! Hell, d'you think I want to be crep' up on in the dark?"

"No one to creep up on you, fool! You're safe as if you were in a church. It will take them hours to break in. So get those damned lights on again! How can I give our dear Mrs. Edgehill my farewell blessing properly without being able to see her? I had barely got started!"

"What? Ain't you goin' to take her along, boss?"

"Only parts of her, my dear Peto," purred The Parson into the dark, unable to resist rolling his vengeance under his tongue. "Only such parts of her as are easily mailed and easily identified, like ears and fingers decorated with familiar jewelry. The rest of her, I fear, will have to remain here among the other ruins after our departure." Then his voice hardened once more into tones of ordinary menace.

"The lights! Get after them!"

Peto grumbled something. Then his voice seemed to disappear.

Captain Vindex kept himself well in hand. Talk wouldn't hurt Mrs. Edgehill, and the propitious dark should last a little longer. He was about to steal down the black corridor to take his chances when The Parson barked again:

"Salvatori! Nick!"

From the direction in which Vindex and Kato had come a minute earlier, crunching footsteps paralleled the wall, to stop within a yard of the two tense invaders. And not a match had crackled! There was a muttered curse beside them, a smell of garlic.

"Where t' hell all dese gravel he come from?" said a strange voice. "Yeah, boss, whatcher want?"

Then, as the unseen Salvatori took a step forward, the first match snapped alive under his foot. In the tiny glow before he trod it out he showed like a denser shadow. Kato darted silently at the shadow's throat. His fingers hooked around a thick neck and both iron thumbs dug into the man's unprotected throat, just above the collar bone. With his larynx instantly crushed in, the luckless gangster had no chance to utter a sound, no power even to attempt a struggle. Kato eased him slowly down, a dead man as soon as he was on his back.

"Nick!" barked The Parson again, ominously.

"Yeah, boss—comin'," growled Captain Vindex in stolen accents. And with Kato he walked boldly toward the welcome summons.

BUT THE PARSON, too, had felt the matches underfoot; and had found one. Just as they reached him he struck it on the wall. With a yell of astounded fury he dropped the match and leaped sideways just as Captain Vindex fired. Kato snatched Captain Vindex, to jerk him in through the open door at which The Parson had been standing, while darkness again covered the latter's hasty escape.

"Plenty hell to pay now," whispered Kato, as he softly closed the door. "But I think kidnap lady are discover. This

are room Honorable Parson emerge out of when interrupt'
in blessing."

Kato struck a match, found a heavy wooden chair and
jammed it under the doorknob. On a small table stood a
candle. He lit it.

Captain Vindex snatched it up and held it high. Over
in a far corner of the chamber was a cot and on the cot,
covered with a dirty blanket, lay a silent little form. He
went over to it and winced as he looked down. From the
small, pale face, shadowed by a mass of tumbled hair, dark
eyes looked up at him. Eyes dark with scorn and loathing
eye filled with hopeless grief and resignation.

"Mrs. Edgehill!" he said huskily.

Her pale lips opened. "Kill me. Or do what you said at
the door. I heard you. But you can't hurt me any more. You
killed my heart and my soul yesterday when you told me—"

Her eyes closed for a moment. Then she opened them
and looked through him, no longer at him. "But God will
punish you—for him—for them—for me!"

He leaned over her, appalled. "Mrs. Edgehill!"

She began to tremble violently. She tried to speak. Then
she fainted. He made sure it was nothing worse and slowly
straightened up. Suddenly he noticed something at the
foot of the bed. He lifted that end of the blanket. "Good
God!" he exploded.

"Are dead?" stared Kato.

Captain Vindex shook his head. "No. But she's taped
to the iron bedstead. She hasn't been able to stir for days."

"You scare her good," Kato nodded. "She seeing Honorable Parson like before. Better you show her when she
come to."

With an exclamation of anger and disgust Captain Vindex tore at his forgotten make-up and flung its fragments to the floor. He scrubbed at his face violently with a wet rag. Then he returned to look at Mrs. Edgehill. She seemed to be in a deep coma.

"We wait," said Kato. "They come get us, we shoot. Then we pick up lady and walk away with."

Captain Vindex shook his head. "Very simple, but it wouldn't do. She'd get a bullet herself. The Parson would see to that... No, open the door, Kato. I'm going hunting."

Kato shrilled fierce expostulation, but Captain Vindex frowned him down. "Wait here till they repair damages and organize to blast us through the door? Be yourself, Kato!" he commanded. "I'm going, and you're staying to protect her. Cut the tape and try to start the circulation. She couldn't walk, now. If I don't come back, and they do— shoot her yourself before you die. You understand?"

"I understand," said the little Japanese, his face wooden. "I stay." He unblocked the door, opened it a crack, looked out and listened. "All are clear. If you die, she die, I die. *Sayonara!*"

11

THE DARK DEATH

THE CORRIDOR WAS as black as before; Captain Vindex moved to the right cautiously and silently in his stocking feet, a gun in his right hand, feeling his way by the wall with his left. This place was no common country hide-out, it was a regular hotel. And it might be staffed with a dozen gunmen for all he knew. All he could do would be to take them unawares, one by one if possible, before they made lights anywhere.

It was a plan that commended itself to fate, apparently, for it began to work at once. Just as his left hand reached the angle of a wall at a corner, his knees bumped into somebody's body crouching on the floor. His finger tightened on the trigger and his lips on a prayer that Heaven might guide the bullet.

"Jeeze!" grunted a voice. "That you, Peto? You scared the guts out o' me!"

Captain Vindex relaxed. "Yes—what's doin'?" he answered, covering his voice and his perturbation in a hoarse whisper.

"Hell knows!" gritted the invisible gangster. "Nobody darst to strike a match. Two of us gone—Nick roun' the corner with his tongue stickin' out, an' Monty with his head caved in. That leaves jus' me an' you an' Black John. Three of us! Gawd, I don't mind a war, but I like to look at it!"

"Where's The Parson?"

"Yeah, there's somethin' else too," returned the other man uneasily. "He went down below to fix things an' light the fuse to that bowlful o' nitro down in the basement. There's cops in the warehouse, blockin' us that way. We got to take to the ol' dry sewer—them that's left of us! He said he'd whistle when it's time—that it'll burn for fifteen minutes! I hope to Gawd he knows his fuses! *Look! What's that?*"

There was a tiny crackle and a flicker not twenty feet away up the right hand corridor. One of Kato's matches! It was answered by the blast of an automatic even nearer, to their left. And from where the match had died another gun vomited jets of reddish flame. There was a clatter of steel on stone, then silence.

Captain Vindex and his unseen neighbor huddled together, motionless. Finally the latter whispered:

"See? That's the way it is. One o' them damn matches started that, an' everybody's got the jitters! Come, le's take a chance, Peto. You game? Soun's to me like they both got it!"

They crawled quietly around the corner, Captain Vindex keeping to the left, a foot back of his companion. As they reached the lifeless obstruction the gangster struck a careful match, cupping it in his hand.

"Hell, it's Black John!" he murmured. "He took it right in the puss! Well, now—"

He picked up Black John's empty gat and tossed it through the dark. It fell with a rousing clatter, which seemed to interest nobody.

"I guess that guy got it too! Must be the guy that came after The Parson! Le's take a look, huh?"

With no little nerve for a man in such a spot, The Parson's rod led the way on his stomach, Captain Vindex following with increased caution and preparedness. The living gunman tested the dead one with a touch. Then he struck another match.

"Jeeze, it—it's Peto!" he gaped, staring down at the snarling face, the forgotten match in his fingers blazing higher. Then his wits came back to him and he whipped his head around.

"You—who—"

He said no more. Captain Vindex's gun crashed down on his skull, and he fell across Peto's body.

Captain Vindex stood up and counted, carefully. Two, four, five! If this latest dead man had told the truth, he himself had been the last of them. Except for The Parson, down in the lower regions of the hide-out.

A SHARP WHISTLE sounded up the narrow stairway off to the right. It pierced him to the marrow. For the moment he had forgotten The Parson's program of blowing up the place upon abandoning it. And back there was Mrs. Edgehill and Kato!

Captain Vindex rushed blindly back down the first corridor and nearly into a bullet out of Kato's gun as he pounded on the door he had so lately issued from. Kato, opening, checked himself just in time.

"They're gone, dead," rasped Captain Vindex with a white face. "But The Parson's going to dynamite the hide-out! Quick, get going!"

Captain Vindex snatched Mrs. Edgehill into his arms.

She was still unconscious. "Back to where we came into the damn place," he gritted. "It's farthest away, and the best shelter!"

"I bring mattress," said Kato. "We hang on to stick of machinery. Maybe they nearly got door open."

Up the corridor and to the left, over the bodies of Peto and the man Captain Vindex had struck down, they hastened. Kato struck match after match on the wall as he ran, and flung them aside. They reached the place they sought and struggled with the lever, but without result. It held some secret trick that was beyond them.

"No use," said Captain Vindex desperately. "We've got to take it!" He laid the slender figure in the blanket close against the movable partition, covered it with the mattress and lay over it himself, grasping the obstinate lever with both hands. Kato added the protection of his own body.

Then they waited. With their ears against the wall they could hear faint sounds as of distant traffic—feel periodic quivers that might have been the blows of sledge hammers. But that was all.

Every second seemed a minute and every minute an hour. But at last it came. The stone floor seemed to heave like the ocean; all the air was sucked away; then it rushed back like a whirlwind, filled with wood and plaster and bits of flying stone, while somewhere behind thundered a Niagara of sound.

Deafened, breathless, blind, Captain Vindex clung to the lever with his utmost power, vaguely feeling Kato's desperate energies added to his own. And in front of him the wall swung open into space and light. Hands dragged him through the aperture, and he collapsed.

Gradually his dizziness began to leave him. The jangling din in his ears turned into human voices, and he sat up. Beside the couch in The Parson's study knelt a figure that he slowly recognized as Edgehill's. His wife was weeping hysterically and happily in his arms.

Captain Vindex's gaze roved further. "Where's Kato?" he demanded huskily.

Burns drew a great breath of relief. "Kato? Hell, Kato went out a good half hour ago to watch the cops diggin' over the ruins! Don't worry, Captain Vindex, Kato was right as rain!"

"He saved my life for me," said Captain Vindex simply.

"And you," said Ellsworth in a low voice looking toward the couch, "saved hers. You and Kato must have cushioned her from all the shock. She was amazingly little affected by it."

"Find Kato, will you? I want to see him!" insisted Captain Vindex stubbornly.

But Kato found himself. He entered the door, bowing and hissing apologetically, to go straight to Captain Vindex and hold out something in his hand.

"Oh, please excuse!" said Kato. "I take from your pocket when you not know. But I so afraid we have no chance later. So I help honorable police hunt in ruin, and knowing where to look could find first, thus imprinting prescription on foreheads like usual. Please excuse!"

"Hell's bells!" exclaimed Burns, staring at him. "An' how many did you get?"

"Five. And telephone girl in Royalton are six, Honorable Mandel are seven. Sweet King of Hearts," frowned Kato, "are belong to Parson, not us. So seven are all."

"You didn't find The Parson?" Burns said tensely. "Of course not!"

"The Parson," said Captain Vindex dryly, "escaped alone after lighting his fuse. Through an old underground drain, I was told."

Burns started up. Then he sat back on The Parson's desk again. "Hell," he said disgustedly. "He's miles away by this time. But we'll get him yet!"

MASK OF VINDEX

*The Sack that Comes Hurtling Through the
Sky Holds a Dead Man. And on His Forehead,
Etched in Blood, Is a Mark of Vengeance*

1

MARK OF VENGEANCE

"READ THAT," SAID Captain Vindex evenly, skating the opened letter toward the centre of the table.

Steve Burns, ex-Secret Service, Edwin Thrale, former lawyer, and Dr. Robert Ellsworth glanced sharply at the speaker and then eyed the letter. The mere summons that had brought them to this mysterious camouflaged penthouse on top of the tall office building at Broadway and Twenty-seventh, was sufficient indication of the purpose of their gathering. They were four and they were pledged to an implacable crusade against the snatch racket, for each of them had a personal and eternal martyrdom of blood and tears to avenge.

Burns frowned as he picked up the letter. "Aloud, I suppose? O.K." Then he unfolded it, and read:

> *"W.W. Norman, Esq.,*
> *"United Rails Building,*
> *"New York, N.Y.*
> *"PRIVATE AND CONFIDENTIAL!*
> *"Dear Sir:*
>   *"By a prompt agreement to invest in our enterprise to the extent of two hundred and fifty thousand dollars in cash, you will save*

yourself much future annoyance and regret instead for having
disregarded this offer.

"The insertion in the Personal Columns of the New York Press
of the single word 'Accepted,' followed by your initials, will suffice
to indicate your acquiescence, whereupon you will receive full
instructions for the completion of the transaction. Should you fail
to make such insertion within one week from this date, however,
we should feel constrained to attempt more direct methods in our
effort to convince you of the advantages of participation.

"In the meantime we beg to refer you to Messrs. Cole Edwards
of Santa Clara, Cal., Elijah H. Pinkham of New Haven, Conn.,
M. Hanson Browne of Amarillo, Tex., and to Mrs. Arthur L.
Stotenburg of Toledo, O., in order to assure yourself of the insurance value of this proposition. At the same time we would strongly

advise you to take no other person into your confidence regarding the matter.

"Very truly yours,

"THE CONSOLIDATED PROTECTION COMPANY

OF AMERICA."

The frown on Burns' face deepened as he finished reading. "Well, hell!" he spat out. "What kind of a hold-up game d'you call that? Or are they takin' the toughest egg in Wall Street for a sucker an' tryin' to sell him a gold brick? What's it mean?"

"Hand it to Thrale and see what he makes of it," said Captain Vindex.

"You're going to travel like a piece of parcel post by air mail."

The lawyer read it twice over to himself, weighing it word by word. He shook his head. "A threat in every paragraph, but it's damned smooth. I'd hate to have to prove anything criminal or unmailable about it to a jury. Those names—I've seen them mentioned in the papers."

"One or two of them are as prominent as that of Norman himself," said Captain Vindex dryly.

"But Walter Norman!" objected Ellsworth. "He's a financial wizard and as hard boiled as they come! He's the last man in the world to pay any attention to such a vague piece of idiocy—or to threats!"

"The last man in the world to give up a piece of change unless it's taken from him by force," agreed Burns. "But he must have paid some attention to this letter, or—Captain Vindex, how come *you* to get hold of it?"

"Norman himself gave it to me."

Burns stared. "So? An' how in hell did *he* ever happen to get hold of *you?*"

"Through Edgehill out in Royalton, near Chicago. It seems he's a friend of Edgehill's, helped him back on his feet financially after we rescued Mrs. Edgehill from The Parson."

Burns narrowed his eyes. "So it was Edgehill referred him to you? That's bad! We don't want publicity."

Captain Vindex nodded.

"This is what happened. Norman knew Pinkham of New Haven, one of those mentioned in the letter. He dropped into Pinkham's New York office to ask him about it, and refused to accept the statement that Pinkham was abroad *incognito,* traveling for his health. He knew better. He finally pried loose the fact that Pinkham's family had just received a direct demand for ransom to the amount of a quarter of a million—the same figure mentioned in *this* document."

"Kidnaped!" exploded Thrale.

CAPTAIN VINDEX NODDED. "As were apparently the other three, Edwards in California, Browne in Texas, and Mrs. Stotenburg of Toledo, all also reported to be away from home 'traveling,' nobody knows where. Just as Norman was supposed to discover, so as to draw his own inferences. I verified the facts for him."

Burns whistled softly. "That ransom demand the Pinkham family got, was it signed by the Consolidated Protection Company, too?"

"It was unsigned. It simply told them to start getting the cash together while waiting for further orders. But Pinkham had previously received just such a letter as this one and had gone to his lawyers, who showed it to some private detectives."

"An' that spilled it!"

"That spilled it, at least to Pinkham's partners, who admitted it to Norman. He kept dark about his own letter, except that he went to see Edgehill. And Edgehill sent him to us."

Burns frowned. "Norman could pay his ransom. He's got the price ten times over, an' personally he'd deserve all that might be comin' to him. Except that—"

"Except that it's worth all the rotten money in the world to rub out even one kidnaper!" exclaimed Dr. Ellsworth hoarsely, his eyes aflame and his long strong fingers writhing ominously. "Who knows what those hellhounds who got Pinkham may be doing to him and to the rest of them?

To the woman? Who is she? What is she?" he demanded. "Is she young?"

"Twenty-four," said Captain Vindex evenly. "Stotenburg—her husband—a big auto man in Toledo, stubbornly insists, according to my information, that she's traveling. Although she's near her time."

Ellsworth went rigid. "So was—mine," he whispered.

"By God," said Burns, "Consolidated Protection is right! Is there a clue to be had anywheres?"

"Only through Norman as I see it," said Captain Vindex. "And no matter what you think about him, Steve, don't forget—"

"Me forget?" blazed Burns. "Don't get me wrong! No more'n I can forget the boy—my only son, not six years old—that they snatched from me an' then sent back to me in a trunk—in pieces! If all the kidnapers in the land had but the one head to blow off of them, bitterly would I regret it for not bein' able to pay them up singly an' separately with all the tortures of hell they've hung on me!"

"That we're all suffering," Captain Vindex reminded him in a voice without emotion.

"Well then, in God's name let's go to it. If you can tell us who or what or where is the Consolidated Protection Company! Time's up for Norman tomorrow, if it means what it says about a week from the date of it! What's he goin' to do? Put in the ad an' give us time to look around?"

"No, he's going to let it go. If he's snatched we may be able to get some information as to the membership and whereabouts of the Consolidated Protection Company."

"Yeah? Is Norman going to let us know where the hideout is after he gets there? Send us a post card?"

"Any ideas yourself about Consolidated Protection, Steve?" countered Captain Vindex. "Who would you say might be behind it?"

BURNS STARED. "ME? How should I know? The letter spells brains an' audacity, an' they seem to be doin' a whole-sale business from the way it reads an' what you found out. If you'd asked me three-four weeks ago, I might have said—"

"The Parson!" ejaculated Thrale.

"The Parson?" Burns shook his head. "Didn't we blow The Parson sky-high in Chicago? Didn't we smash his whole mob up for him—croak his Spotter an' his Finger an' his muscle men, besides the big-time shyster that kept him out of trouble? Believe me, if there's any of that outfit left with feelin's to express, The Parson's on the run—an' damned busy keepin' himself off the spot!"

"You don't do him justice," said Captain Vindex.

"Good God!" stared Thrale. "You mean you do think The Parson is the Consolidated Protection Company of America?"

"Merely a hunch. But I propose to try and find out in the only possible way—as Walter W. Norman."

Burns gasped. "What's that? Another one o' those crazy impersonations? If you want to commit suicide, go out on the roof an' jump off into the street!"

"All right," said Captain Vindex. "*You* suggest a plan. Tell me a better way—any other way to find out *in time* who's behind the Consolidated Protection—to prevent the kidnaping of Norman and above all to rescue those other four, including Mrs. Stotenburg, if we can. And to extermi-nate a few more devils and return them to hell—if we can!"

"But," protested Burns, "there's no reason why *you* should always be the goat to stick your head under the axe! Let *me* do it if it's got to be done! You an' Kato could make me up so you wouldn't know me!"

"Not as W.W. Norman, certainly! Remember, Steve, they must know what Norman looks like. They must have been casing him for weeks to find out just how they can pick him up if they have to. And where would you have us take twenty-five pounds off you? Or at which end should we add four inches to your height?"

"Has it occurred to you, Captain Vindex," Ellsworth asked, "that if anything happens to you the rest of us would hardly be able to carry on?"

Captain Vindex shrugged.

"I'm relying on some protection from Norman himself— on his paying his own ransom for me if it comes to that."

"Not that guy when he's safe on the outside o' the fence," growled Burns. "You'd have to put the screws on as if you was The Parson himself!"

Captain Vindex glanced at his watch. "This is cash in advance. He's due here by eleven. In fifteen minutes. Kato went to get and bring him—*and* the money."

He broke off short at the sound of a sickly thud on the wide tiled terrace outside the penthouse. All four were at the windows in a second, but the darkness was almost impenetrable. Captain Vindex flung the door open.

"Careful! Some one got a flash?" Burns shot one. Its rays rested on a bundle in the middle of the terrace, twenty feet from the house. A large burlap bundle. He bent over and fingered it. He straightened swiftly to stare up at the stars quivering through the faint haze. "Ten thousand devils, is it raining corpses?" he said.

"There was a plane! I heard it a couple of minutes ago!" exclaimed Thrale. And at that instant, an unmistakable thrumming came on the fitful breeze that was blowing from the east.

Burns ran around the penthouse and peered into the night sky. High above the North River and against the flickering stars he made out for a second a dim and tiny shape that seemed to be following the night into the west. It vanished and its voice died with it. Burns returned to the other side of the penthouse.

"Damned if there wasn't a plane!" he said soberly as he approached the silent group. "But it must have been one o' those windmills. Because it would have had to hover— Oh-my-God!" he broke off in a whisper.

For he saw the contents of the sack, now slit open and laid flat. In the light of the flash lay hunched on its back the stiff, contorted body of a man dressed only in a suit of bloody underclothes. The knees were doubled up against the stomach; arms were bent across the chest. Both hands were clenched as if in furious protest, and its teeth gleamed savagely from beneath a heavy gray mustache, while its dead eyes glared blankly up into the dark illimitable sky.

And on its white forehead, crudely traced in blood as if by a living finger and now black in the beam of the flashlight, was a large V.

2

TWO MEN ARE ONE

ACCUSTOMED AS THEY were to the sight of death in its most violent forms, coldly and remorselessly as they could deal it out in their fierce crusade against the snatch racket, all four living men stood shaken.

At last Captain Vindex stepped over to a faucet on the face of the penthouse, wet a handkerchief, and returned to wipe the marble forehead clean. Then he spoke.

"So I was right! The Consolidated Protection Company is The Parson!"

"But others knew of the mark—our mark of Vengeance that's been burned into every kidnaper we've overtaken," put in Thrale with legal caution. "Everybody knows of it. The papers have been full of it after every case. It *might* be a mere coincidence; a killing in some gangster feud in which the killers want to point suspicion another way."

"Wrong," said Captain Vindex with cold finality. "Only The Parson knows who has been using the mark against him, though he doesn't happen to know any of us by sight, I think. True, *one* coincidence is no absolute evidence. But mated coincidences are bound to breed certainty and conviction. And number two is that it is *also* only The Parson who knows where the mark started—knows about

this place, I mean. For it was here that he sent his man
Cantwell as Reuben Acton to impersonate him at our first
meeting."

"And this bird isn't a mobster," said Burns, frowning
down at the dead man. "This was no gang killing! This guy
was a high-brow, you can tell by lookin' at him."

Captain Vindex nodded. "Right. He represents either
a threat or a warning or a piece of brutal mockery on the
part of The Parson. And, possibly still a third coincidence
that will kill all doubt as to the identity or character of the
Consolidated Protection Company of America!"

"How?" stared Burns.

"Cover him up. We'll go inside. It's time for Kato to be
here with Norman."

They had scarcely reached the living room before one of
the sidelights began to flash' automatically. Then a panel in
the wall beside the fireplace slid aside without a sound to
show a small circular elevator cage from which Kato and
another man, dressed in a loose coat with the collar turned
up and clutching a black handbag, stepped across the base-
board. The panel closed as silently as it had opened. The
sidelight settled down to its proper business of steady and
unwinking illumination.

The little Japanese advanced and bowed low, smiling and
hissing politely. "Have brought Honorable Norman. Also
large fortune of money in bag, both with great reluctant."

"With force and violence, he means," Norman grated
angrily as he stared at the four men in front of him, now
suddenly masked. His cold eyes narrowed with suspicion. "What are you hiding your faces for? Am I kidnaped
already? Which of you is Captain Vindex?"

"I am, such as you see me," smiled Captain Vindex acidly beneath the silk of his hood. "Nor quite as you saw me the other day, either, even without the mask. I'm afraid you might not recognize me. And let me suggest that should you have the misfortune to fall into the hands of the Consolidated Protection Company you'll modify your tone and your manner, Mr. Norman. It might save you considerable grief. As for the masks, the reason for them, if you want to know it, is that I don't quite trust you. Or your discretion, rather."

NORMAN SNEERED COURAGEOUSLY enough. "But I'm supposed to trust you however, though instead of coming to my apartment as you agreed—after I'd sent my servants out as you required—this messenger of yours turns up instead, half murders my valet, and compels me to accompany him here with a gun in my ribs! In my own car! And with the quarter of a million in cash which I'd intended to put in safe deposit in the morning. I'd like to know what more your kidnapers themselves could have done to me! Why shouldn't I be suspicious?"

"Your valet?" inquired Captain Vindex. "Then you didn't send all your servants out as you had promised!"

"Well, he—he's a man I've had for years," said Norman stubbornly. "I could trust him as I would myself. And this yellow devil killed him—or may have, for all I know!"

Kato hissed and bowed. "Do nothing but little small jujutsu on when start to oppose going of Honorable Norman. Only press on nerve and put to sleep. Are not hurt, this yellow devil being very kindly. But you say bring money man and money here, so I bring."

"I told you I'd call on you or send for you, as circumstances warranted," said Captain Vindex coldly. "And I wouldn't begin by abusing Kato, since he'll have the care of you all the while you're here."

"All the while I'm here? I'm not staying here! I'm willing to get out of the way as you suggested. I'll take a train south to Palm Beach in the morning, but I refuse to be a prisoner to you. You have the money as security for my person. You can turn it over to the kidnapers if you find you have to. But I warn you I shall hold you responsible for it, Captain Vindex, unless you can prove absolute necessity!"

"Don't be a damned fool," frowned Captain Vindex. "I'm planning to take your place as a threatened victim of the Consolidated Protection Company. If you were left at large the whole world would know it, and we'd both of us pay for it very promptly—with our lives. I'm afraid you don't understand what you're up against, Mr. Norman."

"Show him!" said Burns. "We got a first-class Exhibit A outside, no matter who it is!"

Captain Vindex continued:

"Yes. Something has already happened in this case, and I can assure you, Mr. Norman, that the Consolidated Protection Company had a hand in it, though I don't yet pretend to know its full implication. Kato, switch on the terrace lights."

BOTH BULK AND shape of the burlap-covered mound in the middle of the terrace were significant enough to Walter Norman as he was escorted out to the brightly lighted roof. Under the circumstances he would have been densely unimaginative not to suspect that death lay hidden under that coverlet of rusty sacking. He stiffened and paled.

But when he was led around the mound to face it,

when the incongruous shroud was snatched away and the gruesome corpse confronted him in all its horror, the big broker's former truculence and bluster vanished like the flame of a quenched candle. His knees sagged so that Burns and Thrale had to hold him on his feet.

"You know him?" demanded Captain Vindex, instantly estimating Norman's bulging eyes and dropping jaw. "Who is it?"

"He—he—it's Pinkham—Elijah Pinkham," gurgled Norman between retching gasps, as if he were drowning. "Dear God, it's Pinkham!"

Captain Vindex glanced at his coadjutors. "In other words, it's the third coincidence I suspected and spoke of! No doubt now as to whom we're dealing with," he said grimly. "Bring this man inside again and give him a drink. He needs it."

Norman feverishly gulped whisky until the color began to come back into his face. "What—happened to Pinkham?" he asked hoarsely.

"Just what might happen to you if they got you," Captain Vindex replied. "The Consolidated Protection Company of America happened to him! As you know, they kidnaped him. As you saw, he has been returned! He was dropped from a plane on to the terrace in that sack not twenty minutes before you arrived. But he had been dead for many hours before that drop, judging by the condition of the body."

"But why?" gasped the broker. "His people could have raised the ransom—they were raising it. They would have paid!"

"Why?" snapped Burns. "Because he talked! He was

told to keep his trap shut an' he opened it instead! Family, friends, partners, lawyers, a bunch o' private dicks—they all got an earful. Even yourself! Hell, d'you s'pose a smart mob like The Par—like the Consolidated wouldn't be listenin' in?"

Norman paled. "But I—*I've* talked," he stammered. "To Edgehill in Chicago, at least, and here, to you!"

Captain Vindex frowned. "And who else?"

"Nobody else! Not to another soul! I swear it!"

"Edgehill would be safe. And I took sufficient care in my communication with you. About tonight"—He glanced a query at Kato.

Kato bowed and beamed. "Were followed by inquisitive persons as expected. Were in taxicab. But performed successful disappointment upon by foxy, and by ultimate banishment through place you know where at Twenty-six Street. So buffiloed persons undoubtedly still seeking lost ball in grass, like angry gollifer."

"If Kato says you were being trailed, you were," Captain Vindex announced. "Since they were planning to snatch you if you didn't come across in the first place, they'd naturally keep an eye on you night and day. But if Kato says he tricked them, you can trust him. So you're safe here. The devil himself couldn't get you while you stay here."

Norman's eyes strayed toward the handbag on the table. "Wouldn't it be possible to pay them what they asked, then?" he suggested reluctantly. "So that I could be free?"

"Pay them how? Where? Through whom? It's too late now to insert your acquiescence in the *Press* as they proposed. Time's up. So the only way to connect with them would be to go outside and wait until you were snatched—

as you would be unless they killed you instead!—within
the next twenty-four hours. But even if they succeeded in
kidnaping you and managed to collect your ransom, you
might well be returned as Pinkham was. Or not at all."

"What?" stared Norman. "After they'd collected my
ransom?"

"It's safer and easier to collect in advance, of course,"
shrugged Captain Vindex, "for a corpse that won't have to
be returned, than it is to collect for a captive whose keep
and whose restoration only add to the risks of the game."

"But," the broker sputtered, "that's flat crookedness, that's
dastardly double dealing! I shouldn't think anybody—"

"Hell's bells!" broke in Burns in a tone of astonished
admiration. "I never happened to think o' that, an' I'll bet
they never did! Let's tell 'em!"

"And you're going to submit yourself to that hazard in
my place, for my sake, Captain Vindex?" flushed the man
of money, ignoring Burns. "I hardly understand it."

"Don't think you're the only consideration," answered
Captain Vindex coldly. "It's more for the sake of the others,
already in the power of the devil who is on your track.
It's because it's the only way to uncover him. Come, Mr.
Norman, I have my preparations to make and I need you."

AN HOUR LATER Walter W. Norman re-entered the living
room followed by Walter W. Norman!

The three who had been waiting for them, stared. They
were almost literally seeing double.

"Hell's bells!" said Burns with awed conviction, looking
uncertainly still from one to the other. "It's a masterpiece!
Me myself, I'd hardly know—you!" he laid a finger on one
of them. "It's the eyes. Yours are brown!"

"The one thing I couldn't alter," Captain Vindex smiled. "But you'd be surprised how few people actually notice the color or remember it, even between members of the same family. After all, looks being reasonably equal, recognition is largely ruled by personal mannerisms and by expectation. Even a voice can be varied considerably without arousing suspicion, under the right circumstances."

"I see you even got his clothes on!"

"I've got everything of his that was in any way transferable or imitable. Down to a mole between his shoulder blades," said Captain Vindex dryly. "If I should happen to return to New York the way Pinkham did, I might even benefit by Norman's lot out in Woodlawn. Unless he chose to protest in person. By the way, Steve, you'll have to get rid of poor Pinkham. I'd leave him at least as far away as Van Cortlandt Park. But in the open where he'll be discovered as early as possible."

"I'll tend to him right away," Burns promised. "Tonight. But, Captain Vindex, how we goin' to keep tabs on you? How we goin' to hear from you? Where do we fit in this thing?"

Captain Vindex looked at him, some remnant of a long dead emotion waking to strain against the petrifaction of his heart. He looked into the troubled faces of Ellsworth and of Thrale. He looked at Kato, whose oriental features remained as fixed as a piece of wood-carving, but in whose eyes glowed an affection and a desperate anxiety that even Kato couldn't veil.

"You'll get word before so very long," said Captain Vindex quietly. "Either from me personally—or from The Parson."

Norman, who had been staring at himself in a mirror, turned to stare again at himself in Captain Vindex. "By Heavens, I believe you'd even pass with Hanks, my own valet, Captain Vindex!"

"We'll see. I propose to go back to your apartment for the night and then to your office in the morning. You've told me enough to get by with if I use my brains instead of my mouth. I ought not to have to pose long before people who know you too well, Mr. Norman. And Steve," he turned to Burns, "if I have the luck to be snatched instead of being gunned, it'll be because our friend accepts me as Norman and still prefers to collect. Do you understand?"

"Sure!" Burns drew a breath of partial relief. "He'll have to hold you an' use you to get the coin. He'll have to have Norman's own handwriting to prove he's alive an' worth payin' for!"

"*My* handwriting. But I trust Mr. Norman will arrange to have it acknowledged as his if it comes to that," said Captain Vindex dryly. "Though the longer you can string along the matter of payment, the longer I'm likely to live, remember."

"We'll trace it, by God, even if it's mailed in Moscow or dropped on the doorstep!" swore Burns fervently. "An' if— if anything should go wrong, I promise you we'll get that devil an' send him back to hell, ounce by ounce, if it takes till the damn place freezes over!"

"I've hopes of being able to attend to him myself," Captain Vindex said crisply, turning toward the concealed elevator.

3

THE PARSON SCORES

AT THE BOTTOM of the shaft, twenty feet below the level of the street, its other door slid silently open on to a great, square, gray-walled place evidently used as a garage or as a storage place for cars. For, ranged against the rear wall were cars of several types, including even a heavy truck.

But in the middle of the floor stood a big limousine, across the wheel of which was draped a uniformed chauffeur, staring at the blank wall twenty feet in front of him and muttering deep Irish curses. Captain Vindex watched him for a moment and then stepped out into the open, while the elevator door slid silently back into place.

"Ryerson!"

"Sorr!" Ryerson started, then flung himself out of the car, saluting smartly. "T'is yoursilf, Mr. Norman, sorr! I was wonderin' had anything happened to you, seein' as we're in a trap, sorr." He pointed to the blank wall in front. "T'is there we come into this place, but I don't see how we done it nor how do we get out again!"

"I know, I'll show you," said Captain Vindex.

But he didn't move. He stood there, looking about him. This strong Gibraltar was his own. He had bought the building cheap, unfinished, in the year of the panic. The

year after his children had been kidnaped never to return;
when he had devoted the bleak remainder of his life to a
crusade of vengeance against the forces of evil that had
ruined it. He had spent half a fortune garnered on the
stage in completing and equipping his purchase with every
contrivance for safety and for secrecy.

On top of it he had perched a penthouse, practically
inaccessible and so camouflaged that its existence was
hardly suspected even by the business tenants of the
building's thirty ordinary floors. Its sole familiars, his only
comrades in the deadly raids conducted from the tall eyrie,
were Burns, Thrale and Ellsworth, fellow victims of the
snatch racket chosen out of hundreds, and Kato, for years
his faithful dresser and valet; later nurse, guardian and
worshiper of his children: now his own full equal as their
implacable mourner and avenger.

Captain Vindex wondered if he should ever see his allies
or the place again. He wondered what, should he fail to
return, would become of his Cause itself, of which the
building, in a sense, stood as one of the foundation stones.
But he shook the mood from him and turned to Norman's
waiting chauffeur.

"Start your engine, Ryerson."

While the man sprang to obey, Captain Vindex pressed
a button beside the elevator door panel. The whole front
wall turned on a pivot. Its left swung back into the chamber as the base of a great wedge set on one of its smaller
faces, while its right swung outward until the thin edge of it
settled flush against the wall of an auto runway that dipped
beneath the building and connected the two cross-streets.

Thus the through passage was cut off. But from the secret underground auto floor the way was open to the street.

Captain Vindex entered the limousine. "Home. To the apartment," he said as he closed the door.

Ryerson stared as if he thought his master was a magician, but tooled the car out into the main runway, when the magic block of masonry swung silently back into its original position.

THE NORMAN APARTMENT was far up on Park Avenue. The chauffeur drove east to Madison and turned north. Captain Vindex remained alert and observant, but one-o'clock-in-the-morning traffic was light. Only an occasional car or taxi passed them and but two or three preceded or trailed them.

At Fifty-fifth Street, however, a policeman suddenly barred the crossing with outspread arms. Ryerson braked to a stop and Captain Vindex heard the insistent clang of fire engines, evidently running east and west. Two taxis from behind arrived and drew up, one on each side of the limousine, their occupants stepping out, naturally enough, as if to watch the noisy transit of the fire apparatus. Then both rear doors of the limousine were jerked open simultaneously, and two men came through them like bats through a window. Each had a gun held ready.

The chauffeur, deafened by the passing clamor and waiting attentively for the signal to proceed, heard nothing of what was happening behind him. Captain Vindex wasn't taken entirely unaware, because he had been preparing and hoping for something of the sort. But he hadn't expected The Parson to act quite so promptly.

A gun dug sorely into Captain Vindex's ribs even before

the doors were gently pulled to, while another promptly covered the chauffeur through the open glass, its muzzle within an inch of his innocent spine. Both intruders were crouched low on the floor.

"Not a yip! Not a whisper!" hissed the man whose rod was boring into Captain Vindex. "Or else! An' hoist 'em!"

The victim had already had to guard himself against resistance. But he was there to be kidnaped, as Walter Norman, and it would hardly do to interfere with the process. Nevertheless, the hardest bit of acting Captain Vindex had ever done was when he acted the part to the extent of raising his arms out of danger to the other man.

The limousine started at that moment, smoothly, swiftly. The unconscious Ryerson turned east on Fifty-seventh to Park Avenue. Five blocks further north on that broad boulevard, at a point where he had the whole block to himself, he was astounded to hear a low snarl close to his ear.

"Listen, brother, you switch west again to Fifth an' travel through the Park right up to a Hundred an' Tenth, see? Not makin' no noise about it, either!"

The limousine started the first movement of a waltz, which Ryerson instinctively straightened out. Then he jerked his head around to run a cheek bone bruisingly against a stub of cold steel.

"That's right, Ryerson," snapped Captain Vindex from the rear. "Do as you're told! There's nothing else to do!"

"You said it, guy!" remarked the man who was now his seat companion.

"An' get this for yourself. I'd just as quick put a hot slug through the guts of a bozo that's good for a quarter of a million as I would through a one-eyed tramp that ain't worth a nickel! I'd rather, maybe, jus' for the experience. It would be somethin' to boast about!"

"Am I—being kidnaped?" stammered Captain Vindex in his best imitation of the threatened broker.

"Kidnaped?" grinned the gunman from the other corner of the rear seat, his lined gun unwavering. "What a question! Hell, no, we're jus' takin' you for a little ride in the Park. Would you buy if we stopped at the Casino?" he mocked.

Ryerson's Irish blood boiled in him. But the muzzle of an automatic, now pressed steadily against the back of his neck, cooled the impetuous tide before it reached his brain. And he drove his best and most obedient to order, carefully avoiding such bits of broken pavement or other obstacles he could see in order not to jar a trigger finger that he couldn't see.

Half way through the Park he got further instructions. "Pull up in the shadow of them trees, bo, in the dark."

HE DID SO. For half a minute nobody spoke. The only sound to be heard was the faint and distant murmur from far city streets that is never wholly absent, even in the night.

"O.K., Joe," grated the voice of the gunman covering Captain Vindex in the back of the car. "I guess it's all right—do your stuff. Nothing noisy, mind!"

"Slip out o' that coat an' hat," commanded the man behind Ryerson, "an' lay 'em in the seat beside you! But don't turn round."

Ryerson hesitated, loyal and suspicious.

"Do it, Ryerson," choked Captain Vindex. "You can't help yourself. It's the uniform they want, not you."

Furious and helpless, Ryerson tossed his cap on to the seat beside him and shuffled off his coat. "An' do I get out an' walk, too?" he demanded with open truculence.

"Get out an' walk?" mocked the gangster in pretended amazement. "You, that's used to ridin' in a ten thousand dollar heap? Hell, we wouldn't do that to you, brother! You come out for a ride, an' you get a free ride back. I'll guarantee that! Here's your ticket!"

At the last word his hand leaped to his waist, rose with a knife, and plunged it downward between the chauffeur's shoulder blades. Ryerson broke forward onto the wheel with the death rattle in his throat.

Opening the left front door Joe dragged Ryerson's body out to thrust it under the screen of evergreens. Then he returned and put on the murdered chauffeur's uniform coat and cap and climbed in behind the wheel.

Captain Vindex felt like a murderer for having advised non-resistance, though he knew that the chauffeur was doomed as soon as the demand for his equipment was made of him—a sure foretoken of his fate which poor Ryerson hadn't seemed to realize. But the false Walter Norman had been helpless to intervene. Besides which, the sacrifice of one more innocent life would yet be fully compensated if it proved a step toward the full accomplishment of his purpose. That full accomplishment would eventually preserve far more lives than those of Elijah Pinkham and of Ryerson. Indeed, Captain Vindex would gladly have given his own life in addition, could he be certain that the sacrifice would sufficiently avail.

Nevertheless, some sort of protest was required of Walter Norman. "You've killed him, you bloody fiends!"

he exclaimed in a fierce undertone. "What good did that do you?"

His guard struck him across the face with the barrel of his gun. "No dirt out o' you, louse!" he snarled. "Didn't I tell you I was just itchin' to make me a two hundred an' fifty thousand dollar reputation in Wall Street?"

Captain Vindex swallowed both blow and insult. The reference to the amount of money earlier demanded of Norman gave him some assurance that he was to be held for ransom. Unless this hungry killer's yen for blood should overcome him!

From the northern end of the Park the car turned toward the river, and soon the far-flung lights of the big bridge were lined out ahead of them. Joe pulled up.

"Say, Moss," he mouthed over his shoulder, "hadn't you better sink His Millions on to the floor? You can cover him up with a rug. We got to haul up an' pay when we cross the bridge, see? An' any little thing might start somethin'. We don't want no trouble with the cops just now."

Captain Vindex lifted an arm to protest himself, but not too strenuously. Then the stars fell.

COLD AIR AND rough handling helped to bring him to himself. When he had further recovered his senses, he found he was on his feet, although the two gangsters had him by the arms. But it was for the purpose of supporting him rather than for fear of his escape, as he discovered when they let go of him.

"He's comin' out of it," said the man who had killed Ryerson. "Hey, dope, how's it? Somebody hit you?"

Keeping his eyes as blank as possible, Captain Vindex lifted a hand and felt of his head, partly to see if the savage blow had disarranged the special wig that helped out his resemblance to Walter Norman, whose hair was lighter than his own, close-cropped beneath the substitute. But Norman's head being also differently shaped as well as thatched, the wig had been reinforced in places underneath its lining to increase the likeness. It was on such a spot that the gunman's butt had fortunately struck. Despite the additional protection that had undoubtedly prevented more serious injury, however, Captain Vindex could feel a sizeable lump on his own personal skull, and his head was throbbing.

"Jeeze, you must damn near croaked him, Moss," frowned the recent murderer. "He's been out cold for a good four hours! Give him a slug o' what you got on your hip. I'll take one too."

Captain Vindex started. Out for four hours? Damned if it didn't look that way, for daylight was already breaking in the east over piled-up hills which still hid the sun. The whisky revived him considerably, and he began to inspect his surroundings.

Four hours from Manhattan! That might mean up-State, or Jersey, or even Pennsylvania. It depended. The character of the country was too commonplace to recognize. All he could tell was that it was among somebody's foothills.

Norman's limousine stood a few yards away at the dead end of the ghost of an old country road, barely traceable to the open entrance of a little valley. The land about was bare and plainly long uncultivated. Off to the right stood a group of tumbled-down farm buildings, all weathered to a silver-gray. No other signs of human habitation, old or new, were anywhere visible.

"Where are we?" Captain Vindex demanded huskily of his captors.

"What the hell do you care!" chuckled Joe jovially. "This is only the place you change cars for all points east an' west. You're goin' to take another ride, guy. There comes the hearse!" He pointed toward the barn.

Captain Vindex turned to look.

Through the open door of the barn several men trundled out an active gyroplane, its "windmill" already lazily revolving. *That* was the type of plane—perhaps the very plane itself!—from which Elijah Pinkham's body had been dropped to the penthouse terrace scarcely six hours earlier!

Captain Vindex stared, his thoughts whirling. And at the critical moment between blank astonishment and ominous comprehension, his arms were roughly seized by the pair of thugs beside him.

"Come on, guy," grinned Joe, "you're goin' to travel like a piece of parcel post by air mail. There's a hot one for you! But we got to wrap you up good, see?"

DIZZY AS HE still was from the ringing blow to which he had submitted in the limousine before leaving Manhattan, Captain Vindex was yet able to put up a vicious struggle. But he was at a disadvantage to begin with, and with the help of a third man who came running from the plane, he was thrown and bound, hand and foot.

His mouth was stuffed with greasy waste, and was taped to keep it in; though his eyes were left unblinded. Then, to crown his horror and conviction, his body was lifted from the ground and ignominiously thrust into a big burlap sack held open to receive it, and the neck of the sack was tied above his head. The burlap shroud was picked up by its ends and carried, sagging with his weight, to the plane; as he could tell by his rapid approach to the roar of the engine. And there it was unceremoniously dumped into some small compartment; as he could tell by the effect on his helpless bones.

The plane jerked forward, rocked and bounced over a short stretch of rough ground, then lifted suddenly into smooth air.

Captain Vindex had an all too clear prevision of what was to happen to him next. Mercifully or unmercifully, Elijah Pinkham had been killed *before* he had been dropped from the sky to that stone-hard terrace. *He* was evidently to be dropped from the same sky on to that same terrace—but alive!

For a moment his thoughts were a wild confusion that he couldn't disentangle. How his plans, his precautions, his carefully guarded impersonation could so easily have been discovered, he was quite unable to account for. The one thing certain seemed to be that The Parson was more than ever miraculously served or gifted, and that he was at last on the point of accomplishing a terrible and sadistic revenge.

But something else, fantastic, trivial, occurred to Captain Vindex; and if he had had free space to laugh in or free face to laugh with, he would have laughed in sour, sardonic mockery. When his horrified friends opened this second sack fallen on the penthouse terrace to find that it was he himself who had returned, at least they would find on him no evidence of The Parson's latest and most insolent defiance. The Parson's punks had forgotten to set the Stamp of Vengeance on his forehead.

4

DOUBLE MURDER

"GERMAN TROOPS SAID to be massing on the Polish border," continued the *Daily Events* broadcast from the loud speaker in the corner of the living room. "Looks like the match that will touch off the big European powder magazine—"

"To hell with the Dutch an' the Poles an' the whole shootin' match!" broke in Burns harshly. "It's nearly ten o'clock an' we haven't had a word. Kato! Shut that damn fool off an' give the cops a chance again!"

Kato prepared to switch over to the short wave police signal system when Burns hastily halted him. The *Daily Events* broadcast was changing its tune.

"Wait! Wait! Here's a couple of red-hot home news flashes, folks. A real sensation, right from Manhattan— and let New Haven listen in! Two dead bodies, found miles apart early this morning, have just been identified and point to a crime worse than murder! The first one, discovered up in Van Cortlandt Park, is the corpse of Elijah H. Pinkham, millionaire New Haven stocking manufacturer, dressed only in its underclothes and with every bone broken as if it had been dropped from the Washington Monument! And listen! Mr. Pinkham's New York office admits he was kidnaped over a week ago, and that a tremendous ransom was secretly paid for his return only yesterday afternoon!"

Norman's eyes were popping out of his pale face. "Paid!" he sputtered. "They'd already—" Burns quenched him with a look.

"—other body," the metal voice blared on, "found in Central Park and also partly unclothed, belongs to another millionaire, Walter W. Norman of Park Avenue and Wall Street, the well known banker and broker! Not his own body, I mean, but that of his chauffeur, stabbed in the back right straight through to the heart!—Mr. Norman himself, however, is mysteriously missing, and so is his car, which the unfortunate chauffeur was said to be driving! The coincidence suggests a gigantic kidnaping plot directed against the richest men in the east, and police headquarters everywhere are buzzing like beehives!—That's all so far, but the minute there's more you'll get it immediately on the air through the popular *Daily Events* broadcast!"

Burns, his face set and his eyes glowing, ground out an oath. "They got Captain Vindex before he reached your apartment," he said to Norman.

The broker gibbered. "My God! Ryerson—murdered! Oh, my God!"

Suddenly Burns raised a hand. He had still been listening with one ear to the official short wave broadcast, and now it caught his full attention.

"All cars—all stations," it was repeating, "watch out for dark blue, twelve-cylinder De Soto limousine, license B-two-six-double-O-eight, wire wheels, two spares, driver probably wearing gray whipcord, blue-striped uniform coat and cap taken from chauffeur found dead in Central Park. All cars—all stations—watch out for—"

Burns glanced at Norman. "Right?" The broker nodded.

"Well, that's good news," Burns eased his chest. "Tough on the chauffeur, but it tends to prove Captain Vindex is still alive."

"What are we going to do?" inquired Ellsworth.

"That's the hell of it! We got orders to stand by, an' what else can we do? Even if the police dug up any dope, we couldn't ask in on it! Remember, we're as much on the other side o' the fence as the kidnapers themselves. Hell's bells!" Burns pointed at Norman. "We *are* the kidnapers, far as that goes," he laughed harshly. "Imagine us buttin' in with questions about our own job!"

"But I could explain," began the broker.

"Yeah, just enough to be the death of Captain Vindex, an' that's all it would get us!"

"Beg to inquire," said Kato, "when police persons unable to discover victim of snatch but can seize hold upon kidnaper instead, what are next footstep?"

Burns raised his eyebrows. "Next footstep? Who do you mean—the cops? Why, it's likely they'd start handing him the works—the third degree. Bluffin' out loud that they know all about it anyway, so's to trick him into confession. Unless his mouthpiece happens to get there first, of course!"

"You meaning police persons would say what they knew about in connection?" asked Kato keenly.

"To the goldfish? Hell, they'd spill all they know on him, if any, an' a whole lot they hadn't, just to break him," Burns said grimly. "Why? What's the idea?"

Kato beamed. "I though! Idea this—they spill, I catch. How? Because first, who are kidnaper of Honorable Norman? Me! O.K. So I excurse out into open like dumbbell and become arrest. O.K. Police persons then inquire questions. I refuse to knowing English language which otherwise speak and understand so excellency, but listen in very foxy, thus exploring secret knowledge of, if any. Hence might discover track of lost car in the which are Capta'n Vindex, and we go after. You see?"

"I'll be damned!" Burns stared.

"Yes," said Kato. "More further, if are threatened by keeping or by electrical extinction, you can preserve by supplying lawyer to rescue from imprisoning."

BURNS WHISTLED. "WHAT do you think?" he demanded suddenly of Thrale.

"It would force us into the open," frowned the lawyer. "Of course they couldn't hold Kato if we produced Norman, but—"

—"it would mean Captain Vindex's finish, like I said!"

"But what if I demanded silence and secrecy for my own sake?" asked the broker. "I might even be willing—" He glanced toward the black handbag.

"No doubt you could buy a lot of silence by lettin' two hundred an' fifty grand do the talkin'," said Burns dryly. "But you forget the cops have got two sensational murders on their hands, an' the papers will already be yelling their headlines off. You might get by about your chauffeur, but Pinkham's case is something else again!"

"Then what are we going to do?" Ellsworth insisted. "Heaven knows the police won't get anywhere—not without the inside information we can give them!"

"But won't!" declared Burns violently. "First thing they'd do with it would be set it to music for a full brass band! An' then some one else would drop in on us for havin' been tattled to death. *You!*" he glared at Norman. "Meanin' Captain Vindex in your stead, since it would be New York where the beans was spilled. So *that's* out!"

Thrale gloomed. "We're just running around in circles and getting nowhere!"

"So am going somewhere," Kato suddenly announced with stony finality. "Will submit self to honorable police as kidnap person for to try to find about Capta'n Vindex. Shall keep face closed no matter whatnot. Captain Vindex take a chance, *I* take a chance!"

And the little Japanese was gone.

5

THE KEEPER OF MARINERS' REST

KATO EMERGED ON to Twenty-sixth Street. He kept a keen lookout as he ambled without undue haste across the head of the Square and turned into Madison.

Thus he noticed that an empty taxi swung lazily around the corner behind him and drew even, only to drop back again. One quick glance showed Kato that the empty's license number was that of the cab which had unsuccessfully trailed Norman and himself in the broker's limousine the night before! He even recognized the driver's flat features, though he had only seen the man's face through the limousine's rear window when the street lights had fallen on it.

That the recognition was mutual was equally obvious, else why should the taxi be trailing him? Why? Suddenly the answer, the only logical answer, burst upon him. The false Walter Norman must already have been unmasked. The Parson's local henchmen were again on the trail of the real one! But if that were the answer, *Captain Vindex must be dead!* And nothing worthwhile remained but to take immediate and terrible revenge!

Kato stopped short. Turning to the curb he held up a

hand. The loitering taxi driver was taken by surprise. But he quickly responded, gliding close in to the curb.

"Taxi? Yes, sir!" He leaned out to fumble with the door handle as his eyes flashed a lightning look across Kato's shoulder.

The little Japanese caught and understood the ocular gesture. So there was another one of them behind him? Good! That would make *two* first victims to help appease the spirit of the man he had loved most on earth!

Kato hopped into the taxi, apparently oblivious of that shadow that followed him to slam the door behind them both. The taxi instantly lurched forward into speed. Only then did Kato apparently perceive his cab companion. He beamed and bowed as politely as if the intruder were a friend. The intruder was a dark-complexioned youth with a face as hard and as smooth as marble, except for a tiny black mustache pasted to his upper lip.

"An unexpected pleasure," said Kato. "Can take somewhere?"

"Well, I'll be damned!" the gunman drawled in tones that went with all the rest of him. " 'Can take somewhere!' Well, before discussing your courteous invitation, golden-face, let me say that the handle of this stick is really a neat and efficient little popgun, and it's looking at you. All I have to do is touch a button with a finger and you get a pill in the belly that will cure you of all your troubles. Do you get me?"

"Am not so dumb," smiled Kato. "Know already. Can see into."

The other's waxed mustache points lifted, and his handsome teeth glittered. "Wise man from the East, eh? Long as you keep your paws in sight an' don't make any false motions, we'll get along."

"Shall not," Kato gave prompt and sincere assurance. "But beg to inquire, please, what are going to do together?"

"Didn't I mention that?" grinned his seat-mate. "Why, we're going treasure hunting, almond-eyed son of a cherry blossom. *You* are going to dig up two hundred and fifty grand, and I'm going to take care of it for us. Now don't tell me you didn't know it all the time!"

IT WASN'T WHOLLY a surprise, but Kato decided to play dumb until he got its bearings. "Too much money," he said, still beaming. "Sorry, but no have got. Maybe have got forty dollar."

The dapper hood's eyes narrowed. "Come, don't pretend you're taking this for a cheap stick-up, punk. You know better!"

The driver jerked his head around. "Wipe that yellow-bird's nose with the front sight of your gat, Duke! I saw him with his hands on the kale myself last night, only I didn't know it."

The highbrow hood so happily addressed as Duke frowned at Kato. "Tell me he's wrong," said The Duke softly. "You wouldn't try to play me for a sucker, would you, fish face? I might bust right out—shooting!"

Kato glanced out of the window. The taxi was still being skillfully speeded up Madison and was now in the heart of Harlem.

"Maybe you didn't know we were wise to that part of it," the gangster sneered. "But that valet you only half knocked over beefed his head off to the cops this morning about the bag of big money you took away along with Norman last night. The last editions are full of it. And the dumb cops still think you and your mob have got Norman hidden away!" he scoffed. "But we know better, punk, because we picked him up ourselves an hour later—after he'd given *you* the slip, see? But he didn't have the ransom money— the kale he'd already got together for us—because *you* had it! However, we got him safe now! And safe he stays till he buys his way out again with that two hundred and fifty grand, just as the book was written!"

"Oh, good!" exclaimed Kato involuntarily, the words plumping out of a full heart.

The Duke stared. " 'Oh, good?' What the hell does that mean? By God, you don't think that just because he's good for another quarter million it means you punks can hang on to the ransom you stole from us, do you? Don't you fool yourself!"

Kato realized now that it had only been on account of the money that he had been trailed and captured. But Captain Vindex, it appeared, was still holding his own as Walter Norman! At least he was still alive!

Nevertheless, the situation was ticklish. If it still called imperatively for vengeful retaliation, it now required far more sharpness and diplomacy. For Captain Vindex's life plainly depended on his own, Kato knew.

The taxi rumbled across the Madison Avenue bridge into the Bronx, to turn north among the dingy shacks and yards of the Harlem River waterfront, picking its way across areas littered with slag heaps and garbage heaps and the rusty skeletons of prehistoric automobiles. At last it drew up just outside an old abandoned shed at the rear of a long, low, wooden building facing the water—a building looking almost as dilapidated as the shed.

"Where are this place?" inquired Kato.

AS HE SPOKE, an enormous Negro opened a door at the rear of the building and came shuffling toward the taxi.

"This are place where you get off," chuckled The Duke. "According to the sign out front, facing the river, it's *The Mariners' Rest*—better known in the neighborhood as *The Sailors' Thug Harbor*. And here comes Little Nemo, land-lord and proprietor. Hyah, Nemo, help this yellow chry-santhemum out—and frisk him while you're doing it!"

The black giant handed Kato down to the dirt as if he were a baby, grumbling sullenly while he searched him. He tossed the contents of Kato's rifled shoulder holster to the seat.

A short passage led into a long bar room, empty, dirty and reeking with the rank odor of slops and liquor-soaked sawdust. At the far end it opened into a smaller room, windowless, but supplied with chairs and a table or two. On one of the latter stood an old-fashioned oil lamp, adding its fetid fragrance to the atmosphere.

"Telephone in there, Tiny?" asked The Duke.

"Ol' one, on de wall."

"We'll go in there." Standing at the inner door The Duke looked back over the empty bar room. "Bring a bottle and glasses," he said to Nemo.

Hymie came in. Little Nemo still lingered, his eyes on Kato.

The Duke again faced Kato. "Now do your stunt. Call your mob and tell 'em what a jam you're in. And believe me," said the gangster ominously, "you can't put it too strong! If they don't figure you're worth the exchange we begin to work on you. And you'll tell us how to find them."

6

THE MARK OF VINDEX

KATO HADN'T SPOKEN a single word since his arrival with his captors at *The Mariners' Rest*. But neither had he missed one.

Everything had registered, including the conviction that The Duke never meant to let him leave the place alive, ransom or no ransom.

But how was he to prevent it? He had given way to an impulse of vengeful despair when he had put himself in his enemies' power by jumping into the taxi. It hadn't mattered then whether he were killed or not, if he could die killing. Now it did matter!

Kato had no intention of even pretending to inaugurate a useless bargain for his life—a bargain that would inevitably, one way or another, expose his friends either to the snatch racket against which they were crusading or to the police from whom they also had to keep under cover. Yet every minute stalled was a minute stolen from death—a minute during which some bright idea might spring to life.

"What good I telephone?" returned Kato calmly. "I think you kill me anyway."

The Duke's face darkened. "Maybe, maybe not. That would depend. In any case it might mean the difference between a clean bullet and turning this African giant loose on you."

"Suppose they say pay," said Kato. "How could be arranged?"

"I'll attend to that part when we get to it," said The Duke impatiently. "All you have to do first is get hold of them and spill your sob story!"

It was plain to Kato that all his captors really wanted of him was a telephone number to trace! The loose end of a thread leading even beyond the diverted Norman ransom to those chiselers who had dared lay profane hands on The Parson's private and personal business, and who were therefore due to be destroyed!

All at once Kato hissed and bowed and beamed as broadly to The Duke as when he had first had the pleasure. "Good! I try!"

The old-fashioned wall-box was fastened so high up that Kato bent the movable mouthpiece to its lowest down in order to speak into it.

"I likee Wo'th Exchange," shrilled Kato at high pitch. "I likee speakee Missee Lily Fah Ming! You get? Missee Lily Fah Ming!"

Of the three intently listening in, Hymie snickered into his glass. But The Duke, straining suspicious ears to Kato's curious change of voice and pitch, frowned ominously. Then Kato suddenly broke into a torrent of unintelligible squeals and chatter.

"Hey, you!" The Duke roared. "What's that number? What are you saying?"

Kato stopped short, clapped a palm over the mouthpiece and turned an innocent face. "Are Chinese language.

You wish to talk with Chinese person you give telephone lady name, not number. Then you get. But other man are coming in English. Then *you* get."

The Duke frowned uncertainly.

Kato resumed his conversation over the phone, this time in English, and with Steve Burns himself. For he had foxily obtained a round-about connection with the private number in the penthouse by appealing to the special operator at the Worth Exchange who handled old-fashioned Chinatown. A ruse to provide for a possible posthumous revenge without risk of giving a clue to its agents.

"Oh, yes? Good! This are Kato… Your honorable health are well? Am most grateful… Am at most interesting place. Also have something to tell, and must tell with great quickness. So please to listen, pricking up ears very sharp, yes? Then here are present situation." Kato flung a quick glance over his shoulder at the table. The three thugs, sitting very straight, were staring at him, watchful and suspicious.

"Are ready?—Have capture three kidnapers of Honorable Norman," rattled Kato as fast and as clearly as he could. "One snapper, well dresser call The Duke; also rat-like person refer to as Hymie; likewise large African name of Johnsing or Little Nemo, account of great size—"

He whirled, the receiver dropping from his hand to dangle by its cord.

LITTLE NEMO AND the two hoods—even The Duke's keen comprehension trailing behind Kato's rapid flow of volubility, so utterly alien to anything he had expected—were absolutely stunned as its sense broke upon them. Then the giant Negro sprang to his feet with a roar, the table going over with a bang, lamp, bottle and glasses mingling in one general crash.

There was a second of darkness, to which Kato undoubtedly owed his life; for a blind shot from across the small room nearly parted his hair. Then a thin blue flame spurted from the floor. The spilled oil promptly caught fire from the burning alcohol to blaze high in smoke-capped yellow, and the room became even brighter than before.

Bellowing with animal fury, Little Nemo plunged ponderously toward the Japanese, a knife glittering in his hand. Weaponless, Kato waited for him. Then Little Nemo leaped the last five feet and struck.

Never had Kato's native knowledge of jujutsu, never had his early stage training as member of a Japanese acrobatic team, before he had given himself to Captain Vindex, served him better. Ducking under the great arm as it fell, he twisted about, snatched at the wrist with both hands, wrenched it to the right and bore down on it, all in a single motion. The Negro's beef-sized elbow-joint across the fulcrum of his shoulder broke backwards with a ghastly crackle and crunch close to his ear. The agonized giant uttered a wild shriek and the knife clattered to the floor.

Kato, still clinging to the captured wrist, reached out with his left and seized the other, for the moment almost as helpless as its mate. Jerking them both forward he flashed about to face the room again, bent his body, and with a tremendous heave sent Little Nemo flying over his head.

But it was a dead man Kato had catapulted from his shoulders. For just as he stooped, The Duke, prevented before through fear of hitting the Negro, fired a second shot. His bullet struck the proprietor of *The Mariners' Rest* squarely on top of the head. Yet even in death Little Nemo accomplished a neat revenge on his unintentional slayer. For The Duke, in trying to avoid the hurtling bulk, got mixed up with the legs of the upset table and fell heavily, the Negro's great body landing on top of his own with crushing weight.

Backed against the far wall stood Hymie, white-faced but frantically trying to point an automatic. The fallen knife lay almost at Kato's finger tips. He snatched it up, straightened and threw it. And it caught the shrinking hood in the throat and pinned him to the wall, so truly and forcefully had Kato flung it under the supreme stimulation of danger and excitement.

Even to Kato it seemed a miracle. He stood still, breathing heavily, scarcely able to believe what had happened. Less than ten seconds earlier his own life hadn't been worth those same ten seconds!

Then he saw something writhing feebly beneath the sprawled, mass of Little Nemo. He pounced upon it like a cat, to drag a battered and bedraggled object into the clear and to sink quick thumbs into the soft hollow of The Duke's neck. But Kato restrained himself. He mustn't kill the last possible source of further information concerning Captain Vindex—not yet!

THE ROOM WAS fast becoming unbearable. Fire ate into the rotten walls and greasy floor. Smoke already heavily beclouded the increasing flames and thickly clogged the air. Kato picked up the barely conscious Duke and carried him out into the bar. Then he returned for Hymie and Little Nemo, whom he dragged out of doors to the river bank.

Back in the bar room once more he seized a bottle of raw whisky and poured the fiery stuff recklessly into The Duke's gasping mouth. It was an elixir that would have raised the dead, and in a few moments the unconscious gangster choked, groaned and opened his eyes.

"You tell!" cried Kato fiercely.

"You tell! Where are Capta'n Vindex—I meaning Honorable Norman? Where are?"

The Duke might have died both game and uncommunicative had it been of a natural death by either lead or steel. But the crackling of the flames in the next room and the odor of the seeping smoke were too much for him. He made a futile effort to rise. His face contorted in pain.

"Get me—out of here," he gasped. "For God's sake help me out! I think my—my back's broken!"

"I pour all whisky on you and throw you back in fire room if you not tell!" glared Kato murderously. "Where have taken Honorable Norman? *You tell!*"

"Oh, God!" gasped The Duke. "They took him first to—Sweet Valley Farm near Roshickon, Pennsy—old place abandoned—plane comes there—I meet it tomorrow—regular rendezvous—then, flew him to Doc's fake booby-hatch in Ozarks—Smithtown, Arkansas—it's in Boston Mountains—you—"

The Duke's voice died away as his face went chalkier. Kato shook him ruthlessly. "You tell more! What are booby-hatch?"

But The Duke had stopped telling.

Kato glared down at him in frustrated fury. Still, he had something—more, perhaps, than he could have got from the police if he had carried out his original plan. And there was still something else to do. Lifting the limp body he slung it over his shoulder and bore it out to lay it beside the others.

There, with the knife that had killed Hymie, Kato incised upon the three cold foreheads, one by one, the pregnant ensign of his fierce avenging brotherhood—the fatal V with which its every victim had so far been distinguished. These men had been gangsters, killers, kidnapers, devils! And they should know the mark of Vindex!

7

THE HOUSE OF MADNESS

"WELL, SUCKER," **GRINNED** Joe, the callous killer of
Ryerson, "here you are, without a leak or a crack. Wake up!"

Captain Vindex cautiously tried out his stiffened limbs
while drawing in great breaths of cool fresh air and taking
a quick survey of his surroundings. He had been lifted out
of the grounded gyro to be further freed not only from the
sack, but of his gag and his bonds.

Behind Joe stood Moss, the sullen gunman who had
manhandled him in the limousine, and that third man who
had helped the other two to overcome him and stuff him
into the burlap for what he had believed was to be a short
flight to sudden death.

Yes, here he was—wherever *here* was! On a tiny field
surrounded by fantastic mountain shapes. No such rugged
scenery in the east!

Captain Vindex was jerked to his feet. And as he swayed
uncertainly on his feet a woman's soft voice came from
behind him. "Who—oh, who would believe this was my
own poor disordered darling!" it choked, then broke into
sobs.

Captain Vindex whirled. He faced a girl, slender, youngish and pretty even though lacking any sign of makeup. Her clothes were simple and countrified.

"Yeah," Joe chuckled. "This is your man who done you wrong, beautiful. Mr. Walter Norman of Wall Street, meet the calico skirt, Mrs. Nella Willis from Way Back East. You ought to know *her!*"

The girl curled fingers about Captain Vindex's arm.

Even Captain Vindex's ready brain refused for the moment to clarify such a situation as this.

Slim said sharply, "All set! We're moving. Joe, you and Nella can side the punk in the back seat. I'll drive. Moss, stick the gyro in the shed and stay by it. We'll probably be off again in the morning."

Then he turned to Captain Vindex. "Do as you're told—get into that car!"

In the car the girl tightened an affectionate hold around Captain Vindex's arm. "It's only that sweet private sanatorium we're taking you to, darling," she murmured brokenly as she kittied up to his coat sleeve. "It—it hurts me worse than it does you! But you'll love it once you get there."

"I'll say he will," Joe chortled from the other side, his gun ready across his lap. "He'll jus' go nuts over it like a squirrel, a quarter of a million worth!—Jeeze, what a set-up!"

Captain Vindex glanced at the so-called Mrs. Willis in sharp amazement. A sanatorium, she had said! Was that the hide-out? What did it mean?

From the outside it looked more like a penitentiary as they finally drove up to it—an impression which the appearance of two other tough citizens who unlocked an iron gate set in a high stone wall was scarcely calculated to modify.

Two minutes later Captain Vindex was herded into a building as substantial and forbidding as the wall that enclosed it. Joe still officiated at his right, while the girl attached herself still more firmly to his reluctant left.

There were three strange men in a room. One of them, wearing spurs, a star and a two-gallon hat, came forward as Captain Vindex tried to shake Nella off. For she had suddenly pulled down a veil and had commenced a series of strangled moans and sobs behind it.

"Hey, that ain't no way to treat a pore sufferin' lady," he blustered, "if'n she is your—"

Nella herself cut him short. "Oh, *please,* Mr. Harrison," she quavered. "Dearest Walter isn't really to blame, you know, he—he's not quite responsible!"

Deputy Sheriff Harrison colored and backed up, stammering an apology while Captain Vindex listened in stunned amazement.

"Oh, sure, Mis' Willis, I reckon he wouldn't have if'n he was all there. Excuse me! But don't you worry none. Doc' Herne here, he'll git his wits back into him in no time!"

The man Harrison referred to as Dr. Herne sat behind a most imposing desk, every expression of his face screened by a thick black beard and by the tinted lenses of a pair of large spectacles. During that initial sally he had remained as impassive as a Buddha. Now he called the strange meeting to order.

"Sit here please, Mrs. Willis," he said sonorously. "Now, are you sure you wish to go on with this? There would still be time to change your mind about it."

THE GIRL HESITATED, gazing up at the pseudo Walter Norman as if she hated to stir a foot away from him. Then she pressed his arm impulsively, dropped it, walked up to the desk and seated herself timidly in the chair provided for her.

"What the devil is this about?" Captain Vindex demanded in a bewilderment that needed no feigning.

"Calm yourself," replied Dr. Herne soothingly. "Calm yourself, my dear Mr. Willis. You'll know very shortly. In the meantime—"

"Willis? My name is *not* Willis! I'm Walter W. Norman of New York! You must have heard of me! And I've been brutally kidnaped, as you probably also know! I insist—"

"Yes, yes," agreed Dr. Herne blandly. "I quite understand, Mr. Willis, and if you insist we'll call you Walter W. Norman. But just a moment, if you please!"

Mrs. Willis was struggling a little ostentatiously to control herself. "I—I have to go on with it, Doctor Herne," she choked. "It's—too much for me! He keeps on thinking he's that big New York banker he's read about until—until he just doesn't even know me any more! And then," she shuddered, "I—he's beginning to get violent. He—oh, I hate to tell you!" She buried her grieving face in trembling hands.

Dr. Herne cleared his throat. He turned to the rusty little man at his right, whose hair straggled all over his coat collar and whose Adam's apple was jumping with excitement like a monstrous Mexican bean. The Deputy Sheriff was plainly not a party to the conspiracy.

"Doctor Doddy," bowed Dr. Herne with professional unction, "since this commitment comes from Missouri the law seems to require that you, as county medical examiner, and Deputy Harrison as representing the law here in Arkansas, should officially approve it. You are also supposed to approve and countersign these certificates of mental derangement—after convincing yourself of their correctness by a diagnosis of your own, of course!"

LITTLE DR. DODDY almost swallowed his Adam's apple on one of its down strokes. "I—I ain't no great shakes of an alienist," he confessed. "Just a plain, ordinary country sawbones. All the same, I hope I can still see through a picket fence! I seen him an' I seen her an' I been listenin' to 'em both, an' that's enough! Ain't no manner of doubt in my mind he's as crazy as a coot, Doctor Herne, an' I'll take your word for what ails him!"

"I thank you, Doctor. Then will you sign here, please?"

Dr. Doddy proudly scrawled his official signature, and the awe-struck Deputy followed suit.

"So! And now, dear Mrs. Willis," Dr. Herne's voice dripped tenderest sympathy, "you, too, are obliged to endorse the painful document, and then it's all over—except, of course, for the happy recovery and still happier reunion which all of us trust will soon ensue!"

The girl gave a heartbroken little sob as she took up the pen. She wrote with a trembling hand.

Dr. Herne blotted and handed their copies to his official coadjutors. Words and intonation were suave beyond suspicion as Dr. Herne thanked the ingenuous county officials.

Dr. Doddy nodded sagely. "I've al'ays said there warn't no medicine like passivity an' total inanity for settlin' a man's brains when they git addled. No, sir!—Well, Doctor Herne, me an' the Dep'ty's got to be gittin' along. Glad we was able to help you out ag'in."

Dr. Herne closed the door behind. Immediately the girl became transformed, "My Gawd," she said, and now her voice was coarse and rasping. "What a dumb cluck!"

Dr. Herne said sharply; "Bring him up to the desk! Mr. Norman, now it's your turn! Write and sign what I dictate to you! And I give you my word it will be less than the truth!"

"About my ransom?" asked Captain Vindex calmly. It was just the opportunity he had been hoping for. He saw the whole set-up now.

"Exactly! What a pleasure to find you still sane enough to comprehend that much!" said Dr. Herne sardonically. "And in your place I'd address what you're going to write to someone not only familiar with your signature, but who at the same time can and *will* raise a quarter of a million in short order to save you."

"My secretary," shrugged Captain Vindex, scribbling the name. He knew that any such communication arriving at Norman's office would instantly and secretly be sent to the penthouse.

"Suit yourself. Now write as I dictate."

Captain Vindex wrote:

"Do exactly as you are told in the instructions you receive, and as quickly and secretly as possible. If I have to make a second personal appeal it will be with my left hand. A week after that, I shall have no hand left to write a third with.

Walter W. Norman."

Herne read it over carefully and handed it to Slim. "Start the first thing in the morning and get hold of The Duke.

Handle this in the regular way. You did with Pinkham what I ordered?"

"A bull's eye from six hundred feet," Slim grinned.

Dr. Herne nodded. "Then have The Voice refer to that event as a sample of the penalty that will be exacted in Norman's case at the first sign of a trick or a whisper! Pinkham should still be a front page sensation. Take Joe Fundi and Moss along with you."

"O.K., Boss."

Business over, Dr. Herne relaxed. "Before you go into storage, dear Mr. Norman, let me explain the little Comedy of Errors. As this institution operates strictly in accordance with the law, its patients naturally have to be equipped with all the proper medical and legal credentials. And though God, as you have seen, favors us with some of his dumbest creations in the shape of public officials, it is sometimes necessary to supply them with practical eye and ear evidence."

Dr. Herne glanced at "Mrs. Willis," now lolling in her chair, a cigarette dangling from her lips, and chuckled. "And isn't it just as true today as ever it was in Holy Writ, dear Mr. Norman, that Delilah is still the surest bait for suckers?—Oh, not referring to yourself, of course!—Yea, verily, 'The lips of a strange woman drop as an honeycomb, and her mouth is smoother than oil.' See Proverbs Five, Verse Three. Now take this dog out and kick him into his kennel!" he bidded swiftly and fiercely.

Light couldn't have burst on Captain Vindex with more startling or more stunning effect if all Broadway had suddenly illuminated that dusky room. By a single slip, despite his remarkable transformation in looks and manner, despite the disarming advantage of his new and daring masquerade; by foolishly reverting in this triumph of his latest role, to the old habit of capping his deadly humor with sanctimonious Biblical quotations, Dr. Herne had betrayed himself.

Dr. Herne was The Parson!

As Captain Vindex's guards seized him and marched him out of the room he heard behind him an outburst of clear mocking laughter from the lips of Nella "Willis."

8

A SKY RENDEZVOUS

SLIM AND JOE muscled him down the passage to a transverse corridor at the rear, barred off from the rest of the building by a strong grille.

Captain Vindex was led into a cell-like room with an iron cot bolted to the floor, a thin husk mattress and a blanket, and very little else. At one end was a narrow window grated with steel bars.

He was ankle-ironed and chained to the cot. That didn't disturb him. He had feared they might take his clothes away.

He watched dusk turn to dark through the unshaded window until he could no longer see the bars.

Hours later his door was again unlocked to admit Slim with a lamp followed by a big Chinaman with a tray—a giant with the head of a child, little half-buried eyes that glittered, and an old-fashioned pigtail that hung to his waist. Slim called him Sing Song Loo.

After the gratification of his first meal in over twenty-four hours Captain Vindex was somewhat disconcerted at Slim's production of a straitjacket.

"This asylum being run strictly according to law and custom, Mr. Norman," mocked the gangster while Sing

Song Loo buckled on the jacket, "don't get the idea you can escape. Sing Song sleeps on a mat just outside the grille, and—but let me show you!"

Slim went to the window, raised the sash and whistled. There was a rush of padded feet in the dark outside and four great heads were thrust up against the bars, jaws slavering, red eyes gleaming, throats rumbling with frustrated fury.

"Our night patrol," Slim chuckled. "Danes. And vicious brutes they are! Trained not to bark, but that's the *only* inhibition!"

For a good half hour after gangster and Chinaman had left him, Captain Vindex heard the dogs return again and again to his window, whining, snuffling and growling.

Before leaving the penthouse Captain Vindex had equipped himself to cope with captivity at any ordinary hide-out. Underneath his collar were coiled small steel shapes and wires that could command almost any lock. His thick belt buckle was actually a serviceable flashlight. Inside the heel of one shoe was a flat automatic that would fit in the palm of a hand. Inside the other was that little branding iron built like a cigarette lighter, with which the crimson V—that sign of deadly vengeance taken— had already been burned into the foreheads of a few late kidnapers.

But Captain Vindex hadn't counted on being trapped into any such arbitrary stronghold as this; on being officially if fraudulently documented and committed as insane, or on being straitjacketed to boot. He had expected to enmesh himself in The Parson's web; but not to find himself at its very center under The Parson's own eyes and claws. As it now stood he was helpless.

Nor could he hope that his friends would trace him in time to be of service. He would have to help himself before far likelier things happened, such as the revelation of his imposture and the unpleasant death which would certainly and promptly result. Yes, help himself; but *how?*

IN HIS YOUNGER days Captain Vindex had been expert at some of the simpler stage stunts calling for physical prowess and manual dexterity. He had maintained his interest in conjuring tricks and feats of magic and was familiar with some of the secrets of celebrated escape artists.

Well, he had the strength, but could he produce the gymnastics required to work out of a straitjacket?

He could try. Making a series of desperate efforts he suddenly gained the requisite two inches of slack at the shoulder. After which it was only a matter of able squirming. In ten minutes more he had slipped the jacket and sat up to pick the padlock at his ankles. Then he removed his shoes, emptied their heels, carefully unlocked his door and was out in the pitch dark corridor.

There was another lock to be manipulated, the lock of the grille behind which Sing Song Loo presumably lay asleep. Captain Vindex crept toward the grille like a shadow. His fingers lighted on it like butterflies. And the gate moved! It was already unlocked and open!

Finally he ventured to shoot a thin thread of light toward the Chinaman's pallet, which proved a mere huddle of blankets, and empty! He stooped and touched them. They were still warm. Then where was Sing Song Loo?

Undoubtedly within the "cell block," since he had left the grille open.

Softly closing and relocking the grille to discourage interference from outside in case of a racket, Captain Vindex started to retrace his stealthy steps through the darkness. And almost at once he heard the beginning of a shrill, startled cry, that broke off short into a bitter bubble. It was a woman's voice.

Well beyond his own door he found another that was also open, though only by a crack showing a thin line of light. He pushed it gently in. Almost back to him Sing Song Loo bent over a woman on a narrow cot, one of his yellow hands pressed to her mouth. By the light of the handlamp on a table Captain Vindex could see that part of her white face not covered by the Chinaman's hand. Her eyes were wide with horror as she gazed helplessly up at her midnight molester. Her one visible arm beat up and down within the limits permitted by a cord fastened to her wrist.

Some animal instinct of danger brought Sing Song Loo to his full height. But before he could even turn his head his pigtail was seized and jerked backward, an iron palm cupping his chin to reinforce the leverage.

The Chinaman hadn't time to set the thick muscles of his neck. As force faced him to the ceiling at a sharp right angle to the rest of him, a grinding gurgle sounded in his throat. Then there was a dull crack and his great body went limp all over, dropping to the floor.

Captain Vindex stepped quickly across it. But the girl had gone unconscious, both arms hanging loosely over the sides of her cot. He raised them only to find that her wrists were joined by a cord running underneath the cot—a cord so short that he could not bring her hands together; so short that even to rest both arms on the edges of the cot she had to lie flat on her back!

Captain Vindex saw red. He tenderly untied the cord from one wrist, reaching over her to drag it through and free her other arm. Not till then did he regain his reason. He might as well put a bullet through her unless he could supplement his present mercy by accomplishing her prompt escape. But even if he were able to fight his way out of the building with the girl unconscious in his arms—a quite impossible feat—there would still be the dogs outside! No, until he could get help or first make his own escape there was absolutely nothing he could do for her!

THEN CAPTAIN VINDEX groaned aloud. Yes, there was still something else to do for her! With shaking fingers he reknotted about her slender wrist, as loosely as he dared, the cord he had untied. For there would be trouble enough in the morning, in any case, and if she were discovered freed from her bonds besides, The Parson would make her suffer all the more. But Captain Vindex burned with rage while he performed that necessary act.

He blew out the lamp, dragged the Chinaman's body out into the corridor, searched it for keys, relocked the girl's door and finally replaced Sing Song-Loo on his deserted pallet. And there he gave way to a reckless inspiration. Disposing the body among its blankets as naturally as possible, he proceeded to brand the dead Chinaman with the crimson V. After which he relocked the grille behind him and returned to his own confinement, worming himself back into his straitjacket with far more difficulty than he had found in working himself out of it.

Outside in the night the Great Danes commenced a low and lugubrious howling.

Two hours before Captain Vindex woke from the deep slumber of mental and physical exhaustion into which he had fallen despite his shackles and his straitjacket, Steve Burns and the others were staring from the edge of the woods at an abandoned farmstead nearly a thousand miles away from The Parson's stronghold.

It appeared abandoned with a vengeance. At least so far as the house was concerned with its sagging doors and empty window frames. There were no signs of recent use or occupancy even of the most temporary nature. But Burns stopped and frowned as he faced the barn.

"*Them* doors fit pretty damn tight after years of rustin' an' rottin', seems to me!" He tried them but couldn't budge them. Nor was there any other obvious entrance.

Crawling under the barn from the rear they broke into it through the floor. The main door was new-rigged inside with clean wheels on a rail and was fastened with bolts levered into the stone sill and into the beam above. And on the floor itself were oil drippings, while under a trap was a barrel of oil and three large gas tanks.

Burns swore. "A regular rendezvous was right! For that plane, see? Now all we got to do is wait right here for it!"

Kato saw it first. He had spent the rest of the morning at a crack, peering into the sky. The distant speck was swinging in from the southwest on a long, low curve.

"Now listen!" said Burns. "We don't show till he grounds an' they climb out. There may be several an' there may be a scrap. Pick the pilot first an' see that nothing happens to him no matter who else gets hurt, even if it's one of us. We can't expect to have all the luck! But we need that bird to take us to Smithtown—he knows his landmarks!"

"We open doors and hide back of," suggested Kato. *"I take him."*

IT WAS SIMPLE. Slim, Moss and Joe Fundi walked right into it. Kato jumped the pilot from behind, pinning his arms to his body and throttling his jugular, while Joe and Moss went down like logs, never even seeing what hit them.

The pilot's wrists were seized and his arms stretched to their widest extent, while Burns explored his inside pockets. He drew a blank envelope and opened it, and his face hardened.

"Listen to this!

> *"Do exactly as you are told in the instructions you receive, and as quickly and secretly as you can. If I have to make a second personal appeal it will be with my left hand. A week after that, I shall have no hand left to write a third with."*

"It's signed by Walter W. Norman! It's written to Norman's secretary! *Where are the instructions?"* he demanded of the pilot in a frozen voice. *"What instructions?"*

Slim laughed mockingly.

"Ai!" cried Kato shrilly. "But handwriting are Captain Vindex!"

"Who was this for?" Burns glared at the gangster. "Was

it for The Duke?" he guessed. Slim's start of surprise sufficiently informed him. "So he was to be The Voice, huh?"

"Ask him," Slim answered thickly. "You seem to know
him!"

"You'll have a chance to ask him first, brother! He's gone
to hell ahead of you. But you'll be seein' him!" Burns turned
around. "Drag the crate over an' we'll fill her up. Kato, look-
see if you can't find a big, old burlap sack somewheres.
There never was a barn without one."

"Oh, good!" said Kato with enthusiasm. "I find!"

Slim gulped. "What—what the hell for? You—"

Burns smiled slowly. "To wrap you up in, punk, if you
get cold on the way down. Or get—cold meat! That spell
anything to you?"

The pilot lost countenance before he could control
himself, and Burns read him like a book. "So it was you
who dropped Pinkham," he interpreted. "It shows in your
face! That's why the sack, so's we can drop you too, whenever the spirit moves. But from five thousand and *alive!*
Bring some rope too, Kato!"

Thrale and Ellsworth sided the miserable pilot toward
the gyro while Burns followed. At the door of the cabin
he turned.

"Kato? Where the hell's Kato?"

"Are here," answered Kato from outside. He was laying
a double burden on the grass. "Are always danger of fire at
these places, have found. Like place of Little Nemo burn
up so unexpecting yesterday. And house of Honorable Fall,
banker, in Catskills, time of saving little small Perham child
who were snatch. So are better to remove all kidnapers into

open where can be preserve for further reference. This have done as per usual. Make five."

Slim cast a horrified glance at his late companions. Both Moss and Joe Fundi had acquired the red badge of vengeance and of Vindex.

For several hundred feet up Burns saw the barn suddenly burst into a volcano of flame, sparks flying in fiery clouds. He looked at Kato, but said nothing.

9

VINDEX STRIKES AGAIN

"DEAD!"

The Parson stared long at the form of Sing Song Loo, still lying on its side half covered with a blanket, knees bent naturally, an arm thrown out toward the grille it faced. The big Chinaman might have been deep in a lethargic slumber. "Are you sure he isn't full of hop?" The Parson frowned.

Outside, heard faintly through the thick walls of the sanatorium, the dogs emitted another chorus of mournful ululation.

"Cripes, Boss," said Pinkie, who had found Sing Song Loo, "if he is it was enough to croak him good an' hard! He's stiff as a poker. Me an' Al an' Snicker an' Mack was wonderin' when the hell we was goin' to get our Java, so I come back to the kitchen to find out. Nothin' doin', nobody home. So I come out here an' find the Chink this way. I speak to him, then I give 'im a kick—well, try it yourself! He's so cold he's stiff!"

"Turn him over," said The Parson harshly.

Sing Song Loo came over on to his back, the flung arm now up-pointing into the air, the knees making mountains. But his head lolled between his shoulders, his eyes bulged like marbles, and his tongue stuck out between his teeth.

Nella uttered a shriek of horror. The four hoods drew away, but The Parson stooped over Sing Song Loo. With an oath of utter amazement he straightened, pointing down.

"*That!*" he said in a terrible voice. "How came *that* there? And by God, his neck's been broken!"

They stared at the significant V.

"It—it's the Devil's own mark," said Snicker at last, huskily. "But how the hell—"

"And set there by Vindex himself or one of his minions! Which one of you was it?" The Parson's voice was ice, but his eyes, unscreened by the colored lenses affected by Dr. Herne, glowed like little pools of hellfire.

"One of *us?*" frowned Big Al in angry astonishment. "Be yourself, Boss! We ain't crazy just because we're workin' in a fake booby-hatch! Besides, maybe we could ha' done for the big Chink with a gat or a shiv. But *that* way? Nix! He could have broke any one of us in two, an' you know it!"

"Yes, you'd have been afraid to," said The Parson scornfully, piercing them with a look. "But *who* did it, then? Some one from outside?"

Al shrugged. Pinkie, still shaken by his gruesome discovery, jerked a thumb over his shoulder. Outside the Great Danes were ending another dismal moan. "Get by them without poison?" he said. "Not a chance! Though they cert'n'y got *some* kind o' belly-ache!"

"It's him," said Mack uneasily, glancing down at Sing Song. "Dogs always knows when a person croaks, specially when it's a person they know. That's why they're singin'."

"Superstitious fools!" The Parson barked. "Push that grille open. I think you'll find it unlocked."

"Hell, Boss," stared Big Al. "You don't think—"

He put a hand to the grille and pushed it. It was locked. The Parson's eyes widened. Then they narrowed.

"See if his keys are on him!"

Sing Song Loo rendered up his keys in good order. The Parson hesitated, frowning blackly. Then he unlocked the grille. "Take a gander at them," he commanded. "I'll look at Norman!" He waited until Al returned. "Well?"

Big Al shook his head. "Foolishness, Boss. Not Edwards nor Browne. Couldn't be, anyhow. They're old an' they're weak as cats an' they was scared to death of Sing Song. An' the Stotenburg dame, hell, she's sick. Besides, they're all anchored like ships to a wharf. An' Norman, ain't he even got a jacket on?"

"So I ordered! We shall see!"

CAPTAIN VINDEX WOKE instantly upon their entrance. But stirred and winced as if still asleep, secretly swelling his muscles until the canvas was as taut as a drumhead. The Parson glowered down at him for half a minute. Then he roughly tried to force his hand underneath the straitjacket. Captain Vindex came to life.

"Who put that on you?" demanded The Parson. "And when?"

"Your damned Chinaman, last evening," growled the pseudo Walter Norman. "Tell him to come and take it off—or loosen it, at least! My arms will be dead from the shoulders down!"

"Try a little dieting," answered The Parson angrily. "It might help to relieve the constriction!" Thoroughly deceived by the fit of the jacket he inspected the prisoner's ankle-cuffs and padlock, went to the window and tested the bars, let his eyes rove over everything in still suspicious scrutiny. Then the door was closed and locked again, and Captain Vindex heard the grille violently slammed. He relaxed. Well, they had found Sing Song Loo and the mark. What next?

He soon discovered that The Parson's suggestion about dieting had been turned into a prescription. For although during the day his door was several times suddenly unlocked for a hood with ready gun to look in upon him, nobody brought food. In view of such excessive vigilance he decided to lie low until the turmoil he had raised began to die down again.

Captain Vindex failed to appreciate the full effect of his sanguinary stroke of mystification. The Parson, quite unable to account for it, was in his blackest mood, and as sensitive as a flask of nitroglycerin. After a further and equally futile search of the sanatorium from roof to cellar, Pinkie, more disturbed than ever, ventured an offensive suggestion.

"Listen, Boss, there's somethin' too damn screwy about this business! That V stuff is worse'n dangerous—it's bad luck! Didn't they find it on all them that was croaked in Chi when they chased you out o' your old mission? An' even before that—"

With a snarl The Parson shot Pinkie through the head.

Big Al's mouth tightened to a thin line. "You hadn't oughta done that, Boss," he said coldly. "Or you'll have to put the heat on all of us—if you *can!* Because we all feel the same way. Nobody knows better'n yourself what that damned V stands for—sudden death an' plenty of it! Show us somethin' we can hit back at an' we'll stick. But when a big elephant like Sing Song gets his neck-broke an' that

V into the bargain, nobody knowin' who or how, then it's time to hunt us another hole!"

The Parson glared, but kept his hands down. He was standing in the center of a significantly spaced triangle. "Just a bunch of lousy, cowardly rats, are you?" he said.

"We're no rats, we're red hot rods an' you know it," replied Big Al calmly. "We just got some sense, that's all."

"Listen," said The Parson at random. "If none of you did it, who did? Me? Or Nella? Who the hell else was in the house?"

Al stared. "Jeeze," he said softly. "I never thought! Why, Slim an' Jo, of course—last night!"

"What?" said The Parson, a little startled. "Nonsense!"

"It don't seem to make sense," Al conceded. "But didn't Slim an' the big Chink put Norman to bed together? Anybody see Sing Song after that? An' Slim's a bad actor sometimes. Too hot an' quick. He might have tried to cover up with that V."

The Parson wasn't impressed with the theory. But it gave him a handle, and he knew he had been very close to losing control. "You can ask Slim about it when he gets back," he said.

"I will. I ain't afraid of him. When's he due?"

"Three days," shrugged The Parson. "You know he went to meet The Duke and negotiate for Norman's ransom."

"An' that's a long time without a decent cook," suggested Al baldly. "Hadn't I better rundown to Smithtown an' have Hop Lee send us up another Chink pronto? The broad makes a fancy Mrs. Willis, but she don't know her onions from a cook book."

Ordinarily The Parson would have resented even a culi-

nary slur on a lady living in his company. But that recent
threat of mass subordination coupled with the mysterious
killing tempered his emotions.

"No, nor even coffee from ditch-water," he supple-
mented with a hard look at Nella. "Go ahead!"

AT SEVEN THAT evening Mack, on guard at the gate in
anticipation of Al's return, heard the heavens rattling. He
glanced up. A plane was circling high above the grounds.
He recognized the gyro. Its engine was cut sharply and it
commenced to hover directly down.

Landing on the grounds? That was strictly against The
Parson's orders! Mack ran into the open waving his arms
as if to scare it away like a vulture from a garbage pile.
Slim must be crazy! The gyro settled nevertheless, slowly,
like a drifting leaf. As it hit the ground the pilot's window
opened, to be filled with Slim's head and shoulders, goggles
pushed back. He seemed to be wildly struggling for the
controls, though the engine was off.

"Shoot, Mack, shoot!" he screamed raucously. "The
others—quick! For God's sake—"

Then Slim suddenly disappeared, the hot engine roar-
ing as it caught. The gyro bounded forward and into the
air, clearing the wall only by a dozen yards and shooting
off at a high angle until it circled behind a near mountain
top. Mack watched it, gaping like a fish. Then it occurred
to him that Slim should be in New York! He sprinted for
the house, shouting for The Parson.

"Boss, the gyro's back! Slim come back an' he's took off
again—right from off the place here!"

"Are you drunk?" stared The Parson. "Or have you got
the jitters, too, like Pinkie?"

"A-ah, *hell!*" cried Mack with angry intensity. "Didn't I see him? Didn't he speak to me even? Come on out, I'll show you where she run over the ground!"

The Parson's stare changed character. Mack, Snicker and Nella, attracted by the commotion, followed them out.

"Jeeze, there he is again!" said Mack, stopping and pointing.

Even The Parson had to recognize the drumming gyro as it spiraled down above the sanatorium. When it had dropped to about a thousand feet a tiny object separated itself from the plane to fall whirling. The gyro, as if relieved of a burden, lifted and straightened out in the direction of Smithtown.

"Cripes, it's a bomb!" Mack croaked, too frightened to run. But the Thing struck in the middle of the open ground with a dull thud and no explosion.

The Parson and his woman and his three hoods walked warily out and stood over it. It was a big burlap sack, oddly stuffed.

"Cut it open!" commanded The Parson in a low voice.

Mack slit it from end to end and the burlap fell apart.

"Hell!" he gasped. "Didn't I tell you he come back? *Gawd! Look what he's got on his forehead!*"

10

ARNOLD BRENT RETURNS

BEHIND BIG AL, Captain Vindex caught sight of a smaller figure with its shirt tails hanging out, and carrying a tray. He also caught the welcome smell of food.

Big Al again inspected the fit of the straitjacket. Then he turned, though still blocking Captain Vindex's view of the tray-bearer. "Listen, Chink, this man crazy man, you savvy? Bughouse as hell! So all tied up and no can feed himself. You have to feed him, so"—and Al made the motions. "You catchee?"

"I catchee," answered the ambushed oriental gravely.

"That's the idea. An' don't let 'im bite you. When you're through lock door behind you. Then man will let you out through gate. You catchee?" The hood moved toward the door himself, disclosing the individual he had hitherto eclipsed.

"I catchee," again responded the wooden-faced successor to the late Sing Song Loo. His unblinking eyes rested on his dangerous charge with a total lack of expression which Captain Vindex had great difficulty in imitating.

But as soon as the door closed behind Big Al those wooden features broke into so wide a smile that they threatened to split.

"Kato!" said Captain Vindex in a low voice. "*Kato!*"

"The same," beamed Kato, setting down the tray. "Oh, how are glad to see and to discover! Have been seeking ever since morning after, most hard. Now have found!"

"But—how?"

"Were easy," said Kato. "You eat, I talk." While acting as hand-to-mouth purveyor he rapidly sketched the main events of the search for the alleged Walter W. Norman.

"Slim too!" Captain Vindex interrupted at last! "You dropped him in a sack, like poor Pinkham, right here in the sanatorium grounds? Good Lord, no wonder, then," he stared. "But how the devil did you manage to get in here after that?"

Kato grinned. "Were hired. Last night we were at restaurant in Smithtown belong Hop Lee, wondering what next. Man come and tell Hop Lee he want new China boy quick for cook at booby-house of Doctor Herne, for place of boy gone away. Hop Lee say he not know any. I snake up, slip Hop Lee ten dollar, and get inside job. Ignorant persons not knowing Japanese from China!"

"So you walked right into it," said Captain Vindex slowly. "For me! I'll not forget it." Then he smiled, too. "But it's to me you owe your new job, Kato. That other China boy is dead, I got him night before last. He deserved it!"

Kato's eyes widened. "Oh, good! That make seven! So could extract self out of chains and bindings?"

"I can when it's safe to. Thrale, Burns, Ellsworth—where are they now?"

"Honorable Burns, *et al*, are all haunched up waiting to spring like tiger on this place. Are very anxious about. But are afraid to start till I give signal, because kidnapers might kill prisoners before could be rescued."

"A wise precaution," Captain Vindex said dryly, "though being caught in the same trap you'll find it hard to give any signal. Since two of his devils have died here so darkly and with the V on them, it's just what he *would* do. He knows the V too well."

"He?" puzzled Kato. "You meaning Doctor Herne?"

"Doctor Herne is The Parson."

Kato stared. "Oh, *good!*" he blazed out suddenly with fierce enthusiasm.

CAPTAIN VINDEX HAD estimated The Parson's probable reaction quite correctly. After Slim's premature and horrible return The Parson's position had become untenable. Even Big Al, Slim's logical successor as first lieutenant in the sanatorium, assumed the necessity for an immediate strategic retreat with an air of exaction rather than of mere assumption.

The Parson himself had been far worse shaken than he would have cared to admit. That first mysterious killing on the inside had been bad enough. But the second, from the very air, promised open attack from an outside force which had already succeeded in boring from within.

And that force was Captain Vindex! That accursed Vindex who twice before had wrecked his security and robbed him of immense profits! The man who had slaughtered his henchmen and barely missed adding The Parson himself to the roll of dead and branded; but a man he knew intimately as his most implacable enemy, yet whom he had never once seen to recognize in person! To have Captain Vindex in his power for five short minutes The

Parson would gladly have given the presumptive million due from the four captives he was holding for ransom in those prison cells downstairs!

He rose that morning sourly determined to abandon the sanatorium and to make another intermediate disappearance.

He glowered at Nella. "I never realized until I saw you posing as an actress day before yesterday that you could look quite so washed out," he began. "I wondered how long my eyes had been deceiving me."

"Had been deceiving you!" stared Nella, pricked to resentment despite her state of panic. "You mean when I was doing that Dumb-Dora-from-the-backwoods act for Norman? Well, didn't I *have* to make up for it?"

"That's what I was wondering," said The Parson nastily.

"And 'posing as an actress'!" stormed the girl, missing the second insinuation. "It *was* acting, and *good* acting! And why wouldn't it be? Wasn't I good enough to be with Arnold Brent on Broadway his last season? If it hadn't been for his quitting cold and busting up everything I'd have had my name in lights by now!"

"As for your supporting Brent on Broadway," corrected The Parson, "it was for a couple of weeks only, doing bits. And who was it that really broke up the show by peddling your fond employer's children to a snatch gang?"

Nella stared aghast, too astounded to take due note of the oily alteration in The Parson's voice. Then outraged indignation got the better of her, blowing the small rest of her discretion to the winds. "My God!" she trembled. "That from *you!* Who in hell put me up to it? Wasn't it you yourself, you devil?"

The Parson rubbed his hands and glittered softly. "And yet we failed, you remember. And two little children had to pay the penalty of that failure, just as Slim and Sing Song Loo seem to have paid the penalty for having been connected with another of your acts. You would appear to be as unlucky as Job, my dear Nella—a veritable hoodoo!"

Even then Nella didn't see her finish. "Me?" she stuttered. "Me to blame for what's happened? How do you make that out?"

"Alas," The Parson wagged his head, "since you gave occasion to refer to the Man of Uz, my dear Nella, you should also have recollected his own pious and submissive attitude—'Lest I deal with you after your folly, in that ye have not spoken of me the thing that is right'!—See Verse Eight of the Forty-second and *final* Chapter of the Book of Job!"

"Oh, God!" she gasped, shaking from head to foot. "I wasn't—I didn't mean anything at all, darling! I—I'm sorry!"

"That's better," The Parson eyed her coldly. "Now go find Al and send him to me!"

SHE STAGGERED OUT of the room. A moment later Big Al entered.

"For myself and you, Snicker and Mack," said The Parson, "the limousine will amply suffice. Tell Mack to have it ready in an hour."

Big Al drew a deep breath. "That suits me!" Then, "Did you mean to forget the broad, Boss?" he asked hesitatingly.

"Poor Nella!" purred The Parson. "She has outlived her usefulness. She—and oh, yes—the new Chink will go into the discard with our four patients. Put them in the old dry well down cellar. It will hold them all very comfortably. And if you fill it nearly up with coal, pack it down with dirt and put the cover back it will look as if it had been filled up long ago. See that they're sunk without trace, and we'll have no difficulty in continuing our negotiations to collect." He frowned. "If I only had that devil Vindex to drop at the bottom of the pile!"

"If he only don't come back before we get away," Al muttered. "He's got the gyro!"

"And you've got the jitters," said The Parson contemptuously. "If you find a few other rats down cellar—four-legged ones, I mean—don't let them frighten you!"

Big Al left with his ears pink. Floyd Acton, alias the Reverend Reuben Acton, alias The Parson, alias Dr. Herne, shut himself up to destroy the records of the sanatorium and to secrete on his person such identifying papers and trinkets taken from his latest snatch victims as would tend to ensure payment of their ransoms even if the victims themselves could never be returned. The Parson worked fast, shouting orders through the door.

When Al called to Nella from the hall below and told her to bring down her bags, the girl felt enormous relief. She was ordered to set down the bags and come out back.

"Oh, they going too?" She obviously hadn't given a thought to the captives before.

"Sure," grinned Al. "An' you're to stick right by the dame, so's to keep her company where she goes."

He summoned Kato and handed him the keys. "Unlock gate, see? Then go get people an' bring 'em out one by one. You catchee?"

"I catchee," answered Kato. He plodded to Captain

Vindex's cell, opened it, swung the door to behind him. "I think have got to jump-'em off place," he whispered as he unlocked the ankle-irons and began to race off the strait-jacket. "Men all waiting at gate with guns and lady. I are told to bring out these kidnap persons one by one."

"Might be the bump-'em-off place, instead," said Captain Vindex grimly as he stood up to reflex his cramped muscles. Then he divested himself rapidly of wig and color, of the bits of wax and rubber that had helped to make him Walter W. Norman. "If it's the last drink, I'll take mine straight! You stand by me, Kato. Got a gun? No? Then stand behind me!" And he flung the door wide and marched out toward the open grille.

Seeing the accepted "Chink" at his shoulder, Al watched Captain Vindex's first approach without concern. But only for a second. This was another man!

"Hey, who the hell—"

The palm-sized automatic barked and Big Al sank to the floor, still staring. And that petty explosion was answered by an irregular rattle of heavier guns from outside, followed by sharp howls of fear and pain. The opposing armies at the grille stood motionless.

"By God, they've come!" shouted Captain Vindex in a great voice. "They're shooting the dogs!"

WITH A SHRILL battle-cry Kato flung himself head fore-most through the grille in a wild tackle, only to fall flat on his face. For the two punks, Mack and Snicker, had suddenly darted into the main hallway and were sprinting for the front door. Nella followed them, screaming. But at the foot of the stairs she turned and ran up, her breath exhausted.

Captain Vindex, following her by instinct, caught no more than a glimpse of the open door with Snicker and Mack, one on each side of it, firing around its jambs. Then he saw the gyro, its windmill still spinning slowly in the sunlight, the great animal bodies still jerking in the throes of death, and the three men skirmishing toward the house from behind steady spits of gunsmoke. He and Kato were a bare yard back of her as she burst in to Dr. Herne's private living room.

The Parson leaped back from the window to stare at them. And since the girl came first, it was she whom he favored with his initial attentions.

"You little double-crossing—!" he spat at her, punctuating every epithet with a roar from his sleeve-gun.

Nella staggered back on to Captain Vindex, for the moment both preventing his armed reply and protecting his person. But as he let her gently down she looked up into his face.

"Arnold—Brent!" she gasped, her eyes wide with the preternatural vision of the dying. "Oh, my God!—You!" Then she suddenly pointed at The Parson, screaming hysterically with her last strength. "There he is! He—he's the devil who stole your children! Who—had them killed! And I—oh, God, I helped—"

The Parson fired once again, his fourth bullet passing neatly through Nella's head.

"Capta'n Vindex!" shrilled Kato frantically, springing in front of him to protect him, for Captain Vindex stood rooted to the floor like a man stricken by a thunderbolt, staring at The Parson. The dead girl's vindictive revelation—that this monster had killed his children—stunned him.

But The Parson's arm, too, had seemed to become paralyzed in mid-air at Kato's involuntary cry of warning. Both faces were black and were aflame; both were filled with immeasurable hatred and monstrous astonishment. Kato himself, unarmed, was awed, as if heaven had suddenly decided that this duel was to be fought out with unearthly rather than with earthly weapons.

"Vindex!—Captain Vindex!" breathed The Parson hoarsely at last. "And I've had you as Norman. I've had you—" His face swelled as if he were strangling. His eyeballs were starting out of his head. And though his gun hand still threatened only the floor from an apparent inability to raise it, his left crawled slowly up the front of his coat toward his throat, its fingers like the legs of a spider.

Captain Vindex spoke. *"And—so—it—was—YOU!"* But only his lips moved.

Suddenly The Parson's hand clutched at his thick black beard and wrenched at it with a convulsive jerk, tearing it away. The face disclosed was something very terrible. It was distorted into a fixed and ghastly grin—the grin of a carven fiend, gums bared and set almost from ear to ear. And then his other hand began to rise almost as slowly as the left had risen, as if with a tremendous effort.

CAPTAIN VINDEX CAME to life and fired, his own hand shaking.

The Parson's body jumped and quivered, He leaned back against the wall, slid stiffly sidewise, and crashed to the floor to roll face up, still as inflexible as if his evil will had outlived life. His marble eyes seemingly remained fixed on the man who had shot him.

Captain Vindex knelt down beside the body of his more than mortal enemy and took out the little Seal of Vengeance. When it had glowed to a white heat he burned the V into that rigid forehead, long and deep. Then he rose to stand staring down at him, dropping the pocket branding iron to the floor.

Kato silently picked it up and as silently stole out of the room.

The firing downstairs had ceased, and Burns and Thrale and Ellsworth broke in through the door to stop short at the scene before them. Captain Vindex didn't look up.

Finally Dr. Ellsworth crossed the room. "The Parson?" he asked in a low voice. Captain Vindex nodded. Ellsworth stooped over the body.

"Hit rather high," he said, still in that same hushed voice. "But it must have turned and gone straight through the heart. He is absolutely rigid. But that horrible rictus, whew!"

"Well," Burns ventured, "there's one thing sure! The Devil won't have no trouble recognizin' him for a lodge brother from a long ways off."

"And so that ends it," murmured Thrale after a moment's silence.

Captain Vindex came out of his dark abstraction. "No. Not until we release and return those poor people down below."

Kato had returned as silently as he had left. He knelt for a moment beside the still form of the girl lying by the door. "Make twelve," he said quietly, as he stood up again.

"But," continued Captain Vindex, his eyes going back to the cold body of The Parson, "here lies the Greatest Devil of them all!"